I0534428

SECRETS IN WONDERLAND

A LITERATIA NOVEL

G. LEESON

GRACE ABRAHAM PUBLISHING

Copyright 2024 by G. Leeson.

All rights reserved. No part of this publication may be reproduced, distributed, or transmitted in any form or by any means, including photocopying, recording, or other electronic or mechanical methods, without the prior written consent of the publisher, except in the case of brief quotations embodied in critical reviews and certain other noncommercial uses permitted by copyright law. For permission requests, write to the publisher, addressed "Attention: Permissions Coordinator" at the address below.

Grace Abraham Publishing
A Division of Washington Cooper, Inc.
13335 Holbrook St., Suite 10
Bristol, Virginia 24202

Publisher's note: This is a work of fiction. Names, characters, places, and incidents are a product of the author's imagination. Locales and public names are sometimes used for atmospheric purposes. Any resemblance to persons living or dead, or to businesses, companies, events, institutions, or locales is completely coincidental.

Book Cover Design 2022 by Cover Villain.

Ordering information:
Special discounts are available on quantity purchases by corporations, associations, and others. For details, contact the "Special Sales Department" at the above address.

SECRETS IN WONDERLAND/G. Leeson – First edition
ISBN: 979-8-9885385-4-7

SECRETS IN WONDERLAND

CHAPTER 1

I found myself standing alone in a forest. The first thing I did when I'd gathered my wits about me was to see if the pale green dress I was wearing had pockets. It did. In one pocket, there was a note. I unfolded it and read:

My darling, Gia:

How can I ever thank you for what you've given Cooper and me? He is fine, by the way, and sends you his love and gratitude. He did not have a stroke. He was suffering from Lyme disease, and that caused his temporary facial paralysis. He has since made a full recovery.

Your wedding ring is here safe and sound. A Tale of Two Cities has reset, and all is as it should be with the manuscript.

In case you haven't figured it out yet, you're in Lewis Carroll's Alice's Adventures Under Ground. I'll be joining you soon.

I love you,

Matthew

The letter disintegrated as soon as I read it. I supposed it was up to me to determine what to do next—find a mystery that needed solving, I guessed.

Gazing around, I saw a large, yellow-eyed tabby cat perched in a tree. I stepped closer to get a better look.

The cat smiled. "*Eh, bonjour!*"

I threw back my head and laughed. "Oh, Vidocq, you are incorrigible."

"Since you are here, I take it that your plan was successful."

"It was. I'm glad Matthew was able to go home and see his son and that Cooper is all right. Plus, Matthew said he kept my wedding ring as Lucie." I felt my face flush, remembering that when we—as Lucie Manette and Charles Darnay in the world of *A Tale of Two Cities*—married, Matthew had the wedding ring he'd given me engraved with a quote from the book, "*I think you were sent to me by Heaven.*"

Shaking off my reverie, I continued. "And he says I'm in *Alice's Adventures Under Ground*. But he didn't give me any clue as to what I'm doing here. Have you heard of any mystery we need to set right?"

"Not the faintest whisper."

"Wait," I said. "How are you here? The Cheshire Cat was in *Alice's Adventures in Wonderland* but not in Carroll's original manuscript."

He hopped down from the tree. "Take a seat, *ma chere*, and I will explain."

I did as he requested and waited for him to begin. Eugene Francois Vidocq, a once-brilliant criminal who became known as the first private detective and inspiration for the fictional characters C. Auguste Dupin and Abel Magwitch, was a born storyteller. I was just surprised that since he was a cat, he didn't try to snuggle up in my lap before he began speaking. Instead, he paced, flicking his tail in the air.

"You see, Gia, *Alice's Adventures Under Ground* and *Alice's Adventures in Wonderland* are essentially the same story. A mathematician named Charles Dodgson, later better known by his *nom de plume* Lewis Carroll, wrote the original manuscript—and illustrated it himself—for a little girl named Alice Liddell."

As an archivist for the Smithmore Manor Library, I was well aware of the history behind *Alice's Adventures in Wonderland*, but I kept mum and allowed Vidocq to tell his version of the story.

"The *Alice* stories were created in 1862 while Dodgson was entertaining the three Liddell sisters—Alice, Lorina, and Edith—during a boating trip. He gifted the first manuscript to Alice in 1864. In 1865, the story was illustrated by John Tenniel and published under the title *Alice's Adventures in Wonderland*. So, you see, *ma petite*, Matthew was not wrong, but he was not as right as Vidocq."

I smiled. "I'm glad. I'd hate to have been dumped in this weirdo place on my own with no one familiar to help me navigate the terrain."

Holding up a paw, he said, "Weirdo place indeed. You must remember that this story is full of symbolism and that things are seldom as they seem."

"And even more so, I imagine, now that the story is under the influence of the silverfish."

The silverfish are nasty little creatures, Reader, who are bent on devouring classic literature. Where they've begun eating away at the book, the characters sometimes change based on hiccups in the narrative caused by missing elements of the plot. In other instances, the devious silverfish have taken over characters and move throughout the story trying to thwart our progress of solving the mystery we find inside the corrupt manuscript. If we succeed, the manuscript will reset to normal. If we fail, the piece of classic literature will be as if it never existed in our world.

"Ah, *oui*. You are correct." He walked around the side of the tree.

"Where are you going?" I asked.

"*Pardon*, but I must mark the territory."

I groaned. Some things I was better off not knowing.

I gazed around at the forest. It had the appearance of any other wooded area. There were tall evergreens, mushrooms, moss-covered rocks and fallen tree limbs. I needed to be especially careful of where I walked, since many of the characters in *Alice's Adventures in Wonderland* were tiny. That realization made me happy I was wearing white muslin pantaloons under my dress and pinafore.

Was *I* small? I didn't feel inordinately small, but other

than Vidocq, I had nothing to compare my size against. Having no idea where I'd come into the book, I had no clue as to my current stature.

Vidocq returned and gave me a slight bow. "My apologies, *mademoiselle*."

"Vidocq, how big am I?"

"Vidocq believes you to be just right."

"Thank you, but…" I took a deep breath. "Am I three inches tall? Am I my normal size? Am I larger than I think I am?"

"You are the size of a normal little girl."

"Okay. Thank you." It struck me for the first time since we'd been talking how absurd it was to be having a conversation with a cat.

I felt in my pockets, but now that the note from Matthew was gone, they were empty.

"You are perhaps looking for mushrooms or little bottles?" Vidocq asked.

"Yes. I'm not sure when I might have to shrink or grow."

"When the time comes, you will have—"

He was interrupted by a piercing scream.

"What was that?" I asked.

Shaking his head, he raised a paw, indicating I should stop talking and listen.

"…have your head for this!" a woman was shouting. "Guards! Off with—"

Her words ended with a sickening gurgling sound.

"It's the Queen." I took off in the direction of the commotion.

"One must be careful!" Vidocq warned as he sprinted past me.

I arrived at the scene of the crime moments after Vidocq. Based on the clamor we'd heard, I expected to find a gory spectacle. Instead, there was a playing card—the Queen of Hearts—with its head ripped off. No blood. No mess.

Of course, I realized this was *the* Queen of Hearts. As Lewis Carroll had described in his story, the card's arms and legs were at the corners of the card.

Contemplating the scene further, I realized that not only had the playing card's head been ripped off, but the heel of a shoe had ground it into the dirt. Although there had been no bloodshed, this had been a massacre, nonetheless.

"She called for her guards. Did you see anyone running away?" I asked Vidocq.

"*Non.* I saw the same thing as you see now."

"And what do we do next?"

"We look for clues," he said.

"Of course, we do. I'm sorry. I just—" I shook my head. This entire situation was beyond strange. "Can you *smell* anyone?"

"I am not a bloodhound, *ma petite.*"

"Right. Sorry." I walked slowly around the card, or rather, the body. "We must tell someone...the King, I suppose."

"Yes, do that."

"Aren't you coming with me?" I asked.

"*Non*. I think it best that I stay here and see what happens."

"Okay. That's a good idea. Could you point me in the direction of the garden?"

He pointed to a path in the opposite direction from that in which the Queen was lying. "Perhaps?"

With a resolute nod, I tramped off toward what I hoped would lead me to the garden and the King of Hearts.

I hadn't gone far when I came upon a blue caterpillar sitting on a mushroom and smoking a hookah. In the story, Alice had been approximately the same size as the caterpillar. I wouldn't have even noticed the thing had I not seen the smoke from the hookah rising into the air.

Reader, I suppose I should have been more polite, but I didn't have time for niceties.

Bending over, I plucked the caterpillar off the mushroom, placed him onto my palm, and raised him up to the level of my chin.

"Put me down this instant, you giant!" he cried.

"I will. I promise to put you right back where you were, but I must find the King of Hearts immediately. It's urgent."

"Why?" he asked. "Who are you?"

"That doesn't matter right now. We could go through a whole spiel about my not being the same person I was this morning, and that would be truer than it has ever been in my life, but I have to find the King."

"Why the King and not the Queen?" he asked.

"Because it's about the Queen," I said.

I wasn't sure if I could trust this little blue creature. He wasn't particularly friendly in the original story, and he wasn't bending over backward to help me now. But what if he was a silverfish and led me away from the King rather than toward him?

Since one could see silverfish threading through the teeth of the characters they were inhabiting, I asked the caterpillar to smile.

"No!" He seemed to be insulted. "Why should I?"

"Because a smile would make you so much more agreeable looking."

"Then I shall never smile because I am not agreeable," he said. "Put me down immediately."

"Not until you tell me where to find the King."

"The King is in the garden as always."

"Thank you," I said. "Could you please direct me to the garden?"

He inclined his head in the direction I'd been walking.

Thanking him again, I placed him back onto the mushroom.

"There are places in Wonderland where you are too big to enter, you know," he said, sliding down off the mushroom. "You'd better take the mushroom with you."

He was right. I plucked the mushroom and placed it into my pocket. I opened my mouth to ask him if it was the top or the stalk that would make me grow smaller, but he disappeared before I could voice my question. I supposed I'd find out when the time came.

With a sigh and keeping a wary eye on the ground in front of me, I headed for the garden. Would the King believe that I'd happened upon the Queen, or would he think I'd murdered her myself?

CHAPTER 2

I hadn't gone far when I found a long table set with teacups, plates, and tiered trays of small cakes and scones. It wasn't a nice, orderly table, though. Everything was scattered about, and some things were overturned. Melted butter was dripping off one edge of the table.

At one end of the table sat an older man wearing a black top hat. A brown rabbit and a pretty russet and white mouse that reminded me of a hamster sat with the man. They had to be the Hatter, the March Hare, and the Dormouse. In the original story, the Hatter and the March Hare had shouted, "No room!" as Alice approached, and the Dormouse had slept. Although the Hatter and the March Hare regarded Alice with suspicion, they didn't try to run her off; and the Dormouse was alert and inquisitive.

"Hello!" the Dormouse said. "Who are you and what are you doing here?"

"I was walking through the forest, and I found the Queen," I said.

"You're lucky you still have your head." The March Hare slurped his tea.

"Well, that's the thing—the Queen has lost hers."

"Lost her what?" the Hatter asked.

"Her head," I answered.

"Where did it go?" He put down his teacup and narrowed his eyes at me.

"It's..." I cleared my throat. "Someone removed it from her body."

"What a horrible accident," the Dormouse said.

"I don't see how the Queen's death could have possibly been an accident," I said.

"Sit down and tell us why."

Reader, you can't imagine how weird it was to be interrogated by an imperious little hamster! Or maybe you can....

Taking a seat on the chair nearest me and yet not too close to the trio that I couldn't get away should one of them decide to reach out and grab me, I said, "The Queen's head appeared to have been intentionally cut off."

"As I said, what a horrible accident." The Dormouse pushed the teapot toward me. "You should have some tea since you've had such a shock. It will help to soothe your nerves."

I wondered if this Dormouse was a silverfish. Asking the creature to smile would probably be as effective as it had been with the caterpillar.

"Thank you, but I don't have time for tea. I need to find the King and tell him what's happened to the Queen."

"No time for tea!" the March Hare exclaimed. "What a pity! More for me, though."

"And what *has* happened to the Queen?" the Dormouse asked.

"She's been murdered," I said.

"That's ridiculous." The Dormouse raised her teacup to her lips. "No one would *dare* kill the Queen."

"Yet someone has done just that." I stuck to my guns.

"It was an accident." The Dormouse's tone was steely.

"Why don't you think it was an accident?" the Hatter asked. "Isn't everything an accident? Did you intend to come here to this tea party—to which you were most assuredly not invited? If you didn't, then your being here is an accident."

He had a point, I supposed. "You're right. I did not intend to find your tea party. I was looking for the King and stumbled upon—"

"Ah, you see? You stumbled!" the Hatter cried. "Stumbling is an accident!"

I pinched the bridge of my nose.

"You seem tired," the Dormouse said. "You should have some tea and then take a nap. We'll wake you later, and you can look for the King then."

"I must find the King now."

"The King isn't here," the March Hare said.

"I realize that," I said through clenched teeth. "I need

to find him and tell him what has happened. It's very important."

"If it's so important, then why did you stop here for tea?" the Hatter said.

Ignoring the Hatter's question and, thus, allowing me to do so as well, the Dormouse said, "So, you must find the King and tell him the Queen has had an accident."

Reader, I gave up.

"Okay." I stood.

"That *is* what you'll be telling him, isn't it?" she asked.

"How about this? I'll tell him where he can find her and that she no longer appears to be alive," I said.

"You will tell him she has had an accident." The Dormouse straightened in her chair.

"Why is it so vital to you that I tell the King that the Queen has had an accident?" I asked.

"Why is it so vital to you to tell him that she was murdered?" She squinted at me.

"Because I saw no evidence that she lost her head in some accidental way," I said. "Her head was severed from her body."

"There are any number of accidents that could have caused that to happen. Did you see evidence of murder? Was there a weapon?"

"I didn't see a weapon. The Queen was simply out in the middle of nowhere and her head had been torn off. It *had* to have been a murder."

"No. It did not *have* to be." The Dormouse picked up

her cup once again. "How is it that you are the only one claiming the Queen is dead?"

I spread my hands. "Maybe I'm the only one who knows. Hopefully, not by now. But I found her and feel it's my duty to inform the King."

"To make yourself appear to be innocent?" she asked.

"I *am* innocent!"

"No one is innocent," the March Hare said. "That's why the Queen is always shouting, 'Off with his head!' Why would she want to punish the innocent?"

"Good observation, Hare," the Dormouse said. "No one is innocent."

"I did not harm the Queen. I merely found her in the forest."

"If you didn't harm her, then she must have had an accident." The Dormouse sipped her tea.

"Who has had an accident?" the Hatter asked.

I turned and trudged away from the table, ignoring the whispered response of the Dormouse.

At first, I was so aggravated that I forgot to watch my step. Once I was far enough away from the tea party, I guiltily looked down at my feet. Fortunately, I hadn't squashed anything, as far as I could tell.

I'd entered another patch of woods where pine needles thickly covered the forest floor. It was darker here, given the number of trees obscuring the sun. I stopped and looked all around. The gloom made me nervous.

"Vidocq!" I called in a stage whisper. "Are you here?"

There was no response and no sign of him anywhere. I knew he'd said he would stay in the area where we'd found the Queen, but no one could ever be sure what Vidocq might do. And if something alarming had happened, he'd have tried to find me immediately. Hopefully, then, in this case, no news—or no Vidocq—was good news.

I'd met Vidocq during my first foray into Literatia. I'd been transported into the world of *Jane Eyre* as the character Jane. Edward Rochester, who I'd later learn was Matthew, was already in the book world when I arrived. He'd been accused of murdering his wife and was sentenced to death.

Not being a detective, I had no idea how to embark upon a murder investigation—after all, I'd been hired just that morning at Smithmore Manor as an archivist for the manor's expansive library. Plus, I had no phone, no computer, no lie detector, not even electricity! Fortunately, I'd recently read the biography of Eugene Francois Vidocq and was acquainted with him and his crime-solving capabilities.

I'd gone into town and had bought a newspaper from a boy on the street. In that newspaper, I saw that Monsieur Vidocq was in town. I went to the inn where he was staying, and the rest, as they say, is history. Or, to paraphrase Rick Blaine from *Casablanca*, it was the beginning of a beautiful friendship.

One might wonder how Monsieur Vidocq, a real person and not a character from *Jane Eyre*, could appear in not only *Jane Eyre* but also in *A Tale of Two Cities* and *Alice's Adventures in Wonderland*. As I understood it, Literatia was a world of books—all books. Vidocq had been the subject of both fiction and nonfiction books. Therefore, he had freedom to move around in the books because he was, in essence, of both worlds.

As an archivist for Smithmore Manor library, I was of the world of modern-day North Carolina. I could only transport into the world of Literatia through a portal. That portal was typically a book. However, I'd been transported to *Alice's Adventures in Wonderland* directly from *A Tale of Two Cities*. If I could find a portal, or if someone in the library helped me, I could return to Smithmore Manor.

Vidocq had been invaluable to me in navigating my way through Literatia, and I couldn't imagine trying to solve a case here without him.

Standing at the edge of the forest, I wondered whether I should go on and pass through the woods or ease back out and go another way. I wished Vidocq was here so he could provide some guidance. Since he wasn't, I tried to remember the story.

I knew Alice had found the King and Queen in the garden. I recalled that Alice spent quite a bit of time eating and drinking things simply because they had little signs on them telling her to do so and growing both smaller and larger in an attempt to get into the garden, which she'd spotted from a tiny door inside the rabbit hole. But she'd finally entered the garden by going through a tree, so maybe I was in the right place after all.

Carefully walking through the forest, I spotted a drop of water on the ground. I leaned over and could see my reflection. Instead of the blonde-haired girl depicted in Sir John Tenniel's illustrations, I saw a brunette with a short bob, fringe bangs, and brown eyes.

How odd. I'll have to ask Vidocq why I look this way.

I'd only gone a step or two farther when I saw another drop of water. In this one, I could see Cooper, my boss at Smithmore Manor. There was another man with him. The other man's back was to me, but I somehow knew it was Matthew. I smiled, glad they were there together. They'd been apart for far too long.

I heard someone weeping and realized the drops of water might be teardrops. I quickened my pace but couldn't resist looking down into another tiny pool where I saw a man and woman kissing. Again, I instinctively knew the man was Matthew. The woman was definitely not me.

By the time I approached the source of the weeping, I was sobbing too.

The Mock Turtle was sitting on a tree stump crying its little heart out. In case you haven't read *Alice's Adventures in Wonderland* in a while, the Mock Turtle was half calf and half turtle.

Upon seeing me, the Mock Turtle sniffled, wiped its eyes, and asked, "Why are you sad?"

"I saw something in one of your tears that made me believe I might have been abandoned."

"I, too, have been abandoned." It sighed.

"Perhaps we may be friends then." I tentatively moved closer.

The Mock Turtle moved aside and allowed me to share the tree stump.

I sat down. "You're very beautiful."

"I'm hideous! I *used* to be beautiful—all turtle. Now I'm part turtle and part calf."

"That's what makes you special. You have the majestic head of a calf with those soulful eyes and that broad nose, and what a gorgeous shell you have!"

"Do you mean that?" it asked.

"Of course!"

The Mock Turtle blinked, and a remaining tear fell from its eye. I peered into the drop of water after it landed on the ground and saw the man and woman from before. As in all the water droplets, the man's back was to me, but I knew it was Matthew. He and the woman were laughing.

"We'll never have to be apart again," she said.

I burst into fresh tears. I *had* been abandoned. Matthew had someone waiting for him at home, and he wasn't coming back for me.

The Mock Turtle slid off the log and slowly crept away.

"Wait!" I called. "Where are you going?"

"Somewhere else. You are too negative for me. You make me feel depressed."

What was I going to do now? I needed to find a portal and get out of this place. If Cooper and Matthew wanted to save *Alice's Adventures in Wonderland,* they could do it themselves.

"Vidocq is *tres* disappointed in you, Gia."

I heard the voice before the cat's head materialized. "Vidocq! What are you doing here? I thought you were staying with the Queen."

"I was, but your weeping was disrupting all of Wonderland."

"What am I going to do?" I asked.

"You, *ma petite,* are going to get your *derriere* off that tree stump and go find the King."

"I have to tell you what I saw in the Mock Turtle's tears," I said.

"Whatever you saw is irrelevant. Did I not tell you that you cannot trust what you see and hear in Wonderland?"

"Yes, but why then do I look like Alice Liddell rather than the Alice illustration provided by John Tenniel?"

"Because the story was about and for the real Alice," he said. "Like Vidocq, she is part of Literatia."

"So, the image I saw reflected in the Mock Turtle's teardrop was accurate."

He sighed. "Yes. One image reflected the truth. That does not mean everything you saw was factual. Everything about the Mock Turtle is distorted. He was named after a *soup*, for goodness' sake!"

"I know, but—"

"But nothing. Go and find the King."

"What if I've been abandoned by Cooper and Matthew?" I asked.

Rolling his eyes, he said, "If you have, then you and I will cross that bridge when it is beneath our feet, *n'est-ce pas?*"

"Yes. Yes, we will." I took a deep breath. "Thank you."

"You are welcome. I must return to my post."

"How did you know I needed you?" I asked.

"A little bird told me. Now go and find the King."

I wondered if a little bird *had* told him. In Wonderland, anything was possible.

CHAPTER 3

I was still sniffling a little bit as I trudged along staring at the ground.

"Stop your sniveling please!"

Alarmed, I jumped slightly sideways away from the voice, which belonged to a large dodo bird. "Where did you come from?"

"I came from there to here. Or did I come from here to there?" He tilted his head. "No matter. The main thing is that you need to stop your crying immediately. Were you any larger, you might've drowned us all with your tears."

He was right, Reader. In the original manuscript, Alice, a mouse, and a bunch of birds all had to swim in a pool of her tears.

I remembered something else. I'd read a commentary on *Alice's Adventures in Wonderland* that indicated the character of the Dodo represented the author, Lewis Carroll—a/k/a Charles Dodgson—because Dodgson had a stammer. *Do-do-dodgson.*

What an excellent opportunity! I could speak with the author of the story.

Slowing my steps, I turned and looked at the Dodo. At the moment, he was looking up into the trees.

"Sir, who do you believe would want to kill the Queen?" I asked.

"Everyone! And no one."

"Well, that's a big help." I sighed. "If you had to make an educated guess, who would you say might prefer the Queen gone?"

"Oh, everyone would prefer the Queen to be gone because she is mean. Nothing makes her happy, and she's ever so quick to shout, 'Off with their heads!' at the slightest provocation."

"So, which character is the most likely to have murdered the Queen?"

"Murdered the Queen? Why, no one." He shook his head. "What a ridiculous question."

"It's not ridiculous. You just told me that *everyone* would prefer that the Queen was gone."

"Yes, that's true." He tilted his head in both directions before speaking again. "Or if she were not gone, I am certain everyone would wish her to be a benevolent ruler who showed kindness to her subjects."

I was getting flustered now. Did every single character in Wonderland have to speak in riddles? "Please tell me who is most likely to have killed the Queen."

"No one killed the Queen, silly girl. Without the Queen, there is no story; and without the story, there are no characters. Therefore, we all continue on as we must."

"But, Mr. Dodgson—or Carroll—or—"

"To whom are you speaking? *I'm* the Dodo."

"I know you are, but aren't you also...?" Of course, he wouldn't be that self-aware. Would he?

"I am also the Dodo," he said. "And you are very confused. You should go lie down for a few minutes." He lifted his wing. "In there."

Gazing in the direction in which he was gesturing, I saw a tiny house that I hadn't noticed until the Dodo had pointed it out.

"I'm sure the White Rabbit won't mind," the Dodo said.

Checking out the home of the White Rabbit might indeed prove useful. "But how? I can't fit into that teensy house."

"Sure, you can. You have everything you need to do so."

The mushroom. I took it from my pocket and examined it. "The caterpillar told me the mushroom would make me smaller, but he didn't tell me how it works."

"You'll have to discover that for yourself. I've always been the size that I am with no need or desire to change. Goodbye."

"But wait—"

He ignored me and wandered off.

I looked down at the mushroom.

Ugh, Reader, I really didn't want to do this. This was a far cry from sitting in a sauna in order to lose five pounds to fit into a prom dress. Still, I supposed I was going to have to.

Pinching off a small piece of the top of the mushroom, I put it into my mouth, squeezed my eyes shut, and swallowed. It tasted like mashed potatoes with gravy. I guessed that was in keeping with the first liquid Alice drank that tasted like a mixture of "cherry tart, custard, pineapple, roast turkey, toffee, and hot buttered toast." And while that sounds okay in theory, I believe I'd have found it disgusting. I could handle mashed potatoes.

After giving it a minute and realizing I didn't feel any differently, I opened my eyes. Everything around me looked even smaller than it had before. I'd grown.

I pinched off a portion of the stalk, closed my eyes, and ate it. When I opened my eyes, I'd grown again!

What the ever-loving Dickens, Reader?! I thought the mushroom was supposed to work both ways. I was about to start looking for a beanstalk!

"Vidocq! Where are you?" My voice echoed through the forest like thunder.

There was no response from Vidocq. Okay, so he wasn't at my beck and call, but I certainly wished he was. Like Alice, I was going to have to figure this out on my own.

I would have sat down to think, but I was afraid I'd

take out an entire ecosystem. Plus, I didn't dare cry and cause a flood. How terrible it would have been to get sent into *Alice's Adventures in Wonderland* to set the story right again and end up doing the silverfish's job of destroying the manuscript altogether!

The caterpillar didn't tell me anything about the mushroom except that I might need it to become smaller. But I did recall from the book that one part made a person smaller and one part made a person larger.

That was it! It wasn't the top and bottom of the mushroom—it was the sides! I pinched off a piece of the mushroom from the opposite side, said a quick prayer, and popped the morsel into my mouth. Opening my eyes, I saw that I was smaller.

When I'd managed to get back down to the size I'd been originally, I walked to the White Rabbit's house and then used the mushroom to shrink down enough to go into the house.

I was still a little on the large side, but I could move about freely and snoop among the White Rabbit's things to see if I could find anything about a plot to kill the Queen. It was a longshot, I knew, but I was desperate for a clue. Then I could seek out the King, tell him I had found the Queen lying decapitated in the forest, and hopefully provide the name of a suspect.

There were clocks everywhere—on each wall, on the mantle, on a bookshelf. None of them were working, and the silence was unnerving.

That the clocks had stopped made sense, though. It

was widely known that the White Rabbit symbolized time. He was always concerned about being late. Alice had been unable to catch him and make him stop. After chasing him down the rabbit hole, she hadn't encountered him again until she was in the garden with the Queen.

It was fitting that this elusive character and all his clocks were a part of Literatia. After I'd returned from the world of *Jane Eyre*, Cooper had taught me about the history of Literatia.

Cooper was descended from the Gutenberg family. After Cooper's ancestor created the printing press, the Knights Templar tasked the Gutenbergs with the responsibility of safekeeping literature.

Not coincidentally, the printing press was invented in 1440, and there are 1440 minutes in a day. Yet time in Literatia is two percent of what it is in our world. Every day in Literatia is equal to less than half an hour of our normal day.

But enough wool-gathering. I needed to find a clue to who might want to kill the Queen. The most obvious place to look seemed to me to be the bookshelf. Where else could there be a better chance of finding a clue to a mystery involving literature?

The first thing I discovered was the White Rabbit's baby book.

Oh, my goodness, Reader, it was adorable!

There was the White Rabbit wrapped in a blanket and lying in a basket. On another page, he was a month or so older, and he had some toys. Yet another page showed him with his doting older sibling, and later the White Rabbit and his older sibling were with a new baby.

I was so tempted to put the baby book into my pocket so I could linger over it later, but I resisted. This book belonged to the White Rabbit, and it was very personal. So what if he was a fictional character? His feelings mattered.

There was a book titled, "Secrets in Wonderland," whose table of contents listed a wealth of information about Wonderland. I put this book in my pocket, rationalizing that taking this book was different—it wasn't a personal memento belonging to the White Rabbit. Plus, it just might give me a leg up on figuring out who'd killed the Queen. At the very least, it could help me navigate this strange world.

I reached to take another book off the shelf, and when I did so, a panel opened in the adjacent wall.

Gasping, I took a deep breath, patted the pocket containing the mushroom to make sure I still had it, and stepped into the hallway. There was a light at the end that got brighter as I approached.

Reader, I wasn't ready to go toward the light. In fact, I nearly stopped and ran back into the White Rabbit's living room, but then I heard voices.

I crept closer to hear what the voices were saying. They were shouting, "Off with her head!"

This could be it. I could step outside, eat the "big" side

of the mushroom, and grow big enough to apprehend the Queen's killer…or killers, as the case may be.

I stepped out of the hallway and found myself in the garden standing before the King.

"You, there! Off with your head!" he shouted.

CHAPTER 4

As I stood gaping at the King of Hearts, he laughed.

"It's a joke, dear," he said. "Come on into the garden."

"Yes, join us!" The Knave of Hearts came and took me by the arm, leading me closer to the King.

"B-but you threatened to chop my head off," I said.

"Nonsense." The King dismissed my concerns with a wave of his hand. "I'd never do that. The Queen, on the other hand, absolutely would; but she isn't around today."

"That's why I'm here." I extricated my arm and took a sidestep away from the Knave. Even though he was only a playing card, given my size at the moment, he was a particularly large playing card, and I wasn't sure I could get away from him should he decide to detain me. "I discovered the Queen lying in the forest."

"Why was she doing that?" the King asked. "She has

perfectly good beds at the castle and benches and couches throughout the garden."

"You misunderstand." Fictional characters or no, it was still hard to tell someone I'd found his loved one dead. "She had…um…she was dead."

"Are you quite sure?" he asked.

"Yes, sir. Her head…it had been…um…removed."

"I see." He frowned. "You must take us to her."

The guards assembled at his side with military precision.

"All right. If you'll follow—"

"Right after tea," the King said.

"After tea?" Maybe the Queen *wasn't* his "loved one" after all.

"After tea." He nodded. "You wouldn't expect us to embark upon a sad journey on an empty stomach, would you?"

"I guess not."

He looked around. "Someone set a place for—" Turning back to me, he asked, "Who are you?"

"You may call me Alice."

"Someone set a place for Alice!" he called.

The Knave of Hearts and the Knave of Clubs got on either side of me and escorted me to the table. I wasn't entirely comfortable being ushered to tea by two soldiers, but they weren't threatening. The Knave of Hearts even gave a little bow and pulled out my chair.

"Thank you." I sat, and he pushed the chair closer to the table.

Some diamond cards—a two, a five, and a nine—poured our tea into small porcelain cups.

"Don't be shy," the King said. "Fill your plate."

"All right."

I realized I was hungry, and the food looked delicious. There were cherry tarts, bread and butter sandwiches, and scones with raspberry compote. I took one of each and hoped nothing would make me instantly grow bigger or smaller.

"I love bread and butter sandwiches," the Knave of Clubs said. "I'm glad we can have them now."

"And the scones, too," the Knave of Hearts added. "I enjoy the cherry tarts, but they can't compare to the scones with raspberry compote."

"You don't have them often?" I asked.

"No," the Knave of Clubs said. "The Queen didn't like them and wouldn't allow them to be served."

I looked at the King, whose plate was piled high, and he was eating with both hands.

"It's good to be the King," I murmured.

He stopped eating and pierced me with his gaze. "Indeed."

Giving him a brief smile, I resumed eating. The King certainly didn't seem upset that the Queen was gone.

───

AFTER WE'D FINISHED EATING, the King asked me to take him and the guards to the Queen.

"All right." I pointed toward the passageway from which I'd entered the garden. "I came from there."

"We aren't going that way," he said. "That leads to the White Rabbit's house, and it would be rude to be there when he isn't home. Don't you agree?"

"Yes, but I don't know how to get to the woods if I don't retrace my steps."

"We'll get you there." He nodded, and several soldiers got in front of us to lead the way. "Tell me, who are you, and where did you come from?"

"I've already told you my name. I was sitting on the riverbank with my older sister," I said. "I was bored and was considering making a daisy chain when I spotted a white rabbit and followed it here."

"No, no, no—tell me who you *are*," he said.

I decided to throw out the quote that I'd been too busy to use on the caterpillar. "I know who I was when I got up this morning, but I think I must have changed several times since then."

The King stopped walking. "I demand that you tell me who you are immediately."

Now I was a couple of steps ahead of him, so I turned back to look at him. His face still looked kind enough, but there was something in his eyes that I didn't like.

"My name is Alice. My father is Dean of Christ Church at Oxford. My sister, Lorina, is waiting for me on the bank, and I need to return to her as soon as I've taken you to the Queen."

He smiled, and I saw a silverfish wind between two of

his molars. Fortunately, I was able to suppress my reaction.

"Very well," he said. "Carry on."

I wondered if it was he who'd killed the Queen.

Now that I knew he was a silverfish, I didn't want to turn my back on him. I waited for him to catch up to me.

"Tell me about yourself," I said. "You know all about me now."

"Do I?" he asked.

"All the important things anyway." I shrugged. "Do you enjoy being in power?"

"Everyone enjoys being in power."

"I disagree. Some people don't want the responsibility of being in power. They'd rather follow than lead," I said. "They don't want the accolades if they make the right decisions or the consequences if they make the wrong decisions."

The King frowned at me. "That's an astute observation for a little girl."

He had me there, Reader.

"I spend a lot of time with adults." I grinned. "I suppose I am wise beyond my years."

"And yet all you could tell me about yourself was that your name is Alice, your father is the dean of a college, and you have an older sister who is waiting for you on a riverbank."

"What more do you need to know?" I asked.

"I need to know who you really are and what you're doing here," he said.

Glancing around at our surroundings, I saw that we were in front of the White Rabbit's house. "What do you know? We're back where I started."

"Where to now, Your Majesty?" asked the Knave of Hearts.

"I suppose that's up to *Alice*. Where to next, my dear?"

"We keep going straight."

It was difficult to remember where I'd found the Queen. The landscape didn't change very much. At this point, all I really knew was that I'd walked with a Dodo, wept with a Mock Turtle, and been interrogated at a tea party. The Dodo and the Mock Turtle had left the places where I'd found them. I only hoped the tea table was still there, so I'd know I was on the right track.

After walking for what seemed like hours but couldn't have been more than a few minutes, we came upon the tea party just as I'd left it.

"It's her!" the Dormouse cried.

"She's found the King." The March Hare raised his teacup in salute. "Good work."

"Would you care for a cup of tea, Your Majesty?" the Hatter asked.

"As a matter of fact, I would like that very much." He sat down at the table across from the March Hare. "We have walked quite a long way."

The soldiers stood at attention, and I folded my arms across my chest as I waited for the King to have tea. Again.

The Hatter poured the King a cup of tea. "I hope it is to your liking, sire."

Dropping a sugar cube into the cup, the King said, "I imagine it will be delightful. Tell me what you know about our guest here. You've encountered her once already today, I believe."

"We have," the Dormouse said. "She told us the Queen had suffered a horrible accident."

"Yes." The King sipped his tea, and from the expression on his face, he didn't find it to be delightful in the least. "She is taking us to the place where she found the Queen so we can collect her and take her back to the palace to get well."

"I'm glad of that." The Dormouse scowled at me. "*She* made it seem as if the Queen were dead. What nonsense."

"What nonsense indeed," the King said. "As much as I regret leaving such pleasant company, we should be on our way." He stood. "Alice, you may carry on now."

"Soldiers, lead the way," I said. "The King and I will be right behind you."

"What direction, miss?" the Knave of Clubs asked.

"Straight on ahead." I waited for the King to get to my side.

We passed the area where I was convinced I'd spoken with the blue caterpillar. However, he wasn't there, and I was carrying in my pocket the half-eaten mushroom on which he'd sat. I didn't see smoke from his hookah either.

Still, the surroundings appeared familiar. I kept walking.

At last, we reached the place where I thought I'd found the Queen.

"We're getting close," I said.

The soldiers slowed.

"It was right around here. I'm sure of it." I looked at the ground all around me, reminding myself that I'd been bigger when I'd found the Queen. Maybe that was why my directions were off.

"I see nothing," the King said.

"She was lying right here in this clearing." I blew out a breath. "I was larger when I found her. It was before I'd eaten any of the caterpillar's mushroom."

"You're a very wicked girl to play such a cruel prank on us." The King didn't look angry. Instead, he looked smug.

Taking the mushroom from my pocket, I took a tiny bite off the grow-larger side. When my size had increased, the soldiers drew back in alarm.

Having a better view, I was certain this was the place where I'd found the Queen. But she was no longer here. What had happened?

"This is where she was," I said. "I know it."

"Once again, you're a wicked girl," the King said. "We won't be a party to your tricks any longer. Guards, let us return at once to the garden. *Alice*, if that *is* your name, do not follow us, or you'll find yourself locked in a dungeon."

CHAPTER 5

"I should've told those guards that I'd shuffle them and deal them out in a game of solitaire," I told Vidocq when he appeared. "This *is* where we found the Queen's body, isn't it?"

"*Oui*." He turned in a full circle as he gazed around the meadow. "Vidocq is certain of it."

"Then where did she go? She *was* dead, right? You didn't see her get up and walk away, did you?"

"I did not." His tail twitched, and he avoided my eyes. "However, when I came back from checking on you when you were weeping with the Mock Turtle, she was gone."

"How? You weren't with me *that* long. Is there any way she *wasn't* dead? Or could she have come back to life? I mean, this *is* Wonderland, after all, where people can grow and shrink and do all sorts of weirdo things."

"As far as I know, death is final, even in Wonderland," he said.

"Before he accused me of playing a trick on him, that King looked awfully self-satisfied when I couldn't find the Queen's body. Do you think he might've hired someone to take the Queen's body and hide it?" I rubbed my chin. "He could divert suspicion that way. If the Queen were to simply disappear, then he could say she'd gone away somewhere or was sick and in her chambers at the castle or something. He could rule without any interference."

"Vidocq believes you are giving too much credit to a deck of playing cards, *ma petite.*"

"But the King is a silverfish."

"Ah, that is different then. Hold out your arms."

I did as he requested, and he jumped into them. "You expect me to carry you?"

"*Oui.*" He grinned. "Your legs are much longer, and I am a lazy cat. Let us go and look for the Queen together."

"All right." I examined the ground where the Queen had been lying and saw that the grass had been flattened. "Look at that. It appears the Queen's body was dragged away. Maybe the King didn't have a hand in her disappearing from this clearing after all. His guards would have picked up the body—they'd have had no need to drag it."

"Perhaps the King acted alone and does not want the guards to know his business," Vidocq said. "It is dangerous for people in power to share secrets with their subordinates."

"True. Let's see where these drag marks lead us." I followed the trail of flattened grass until it stopped at a gravel path.

I saw no indication that the body had been led in another direction, so I decided to go down the path. Hopefully, it would either lead us to the Queen's body or to the person who had moved it.

The gravel path led to a charming little cottage that was about four feet high. It was white with a blue roof, blue shutters, and a blue door. Given the size, I thought it might be the Duchess's cottage. But unlike in the book, there was no Frog Footman standing at the door. And, unlike in the book, I—as Alice—did not shrink down in order to be admitted into the house. I thought it might be good if the occupants were intimidated by my size. I might actually get some answers that way.

With my index finger, I tapped gently on the door.

A woman wearing a drab housedress and an apron answered. The Cook.

From inside, a woman's shrill voice called, "Who's there?"

The Duchess. Yep. I was correct in my calculation of where I'd wound up.

"It's a strange girl," the Cook replied.

"What's so strange about her?" the Duchess asked.

"She's freakishly large."

Reader, this made me wonder if I should go ahead and partake of the shrinking side of the mushroom, but I decided against it.

The Duchess came to the door to see the giant girl. "Oh, look at that. She's found the cat and brought him back."

Vidocq promptly turned invisible and jumped out of my arms.

"Hey!" I protested.

"It's all right," the Duchess said. "He does that. He'll turn up." She shut the door in my face.

I blew out a breath and tapped the door again.

The Cook opened the door. "Back already?"

"I never left."

"Why not?" she asked.

"Because I'm searching for the Queen of Hearts," I said.

"She doesn't live here," the Cook said. "This is the Duchess's house."

"I know. I am also aware that the Duchess is the Queen's sister."

Upon hearing this, the Duchess poked her head around the open door. "And?"

"And I saw the Queen this morning lying in the meadow," I said. "She'd lost her head."

"Well, that—" the Cook began.

"Tut, tut!" the Duchess interrupted sharply. "Get back to the kitchen, Cook, and finish making the soup!" She glanced back up at me then and said, "We have not seen my sister." And, once again, she shut the door in my face.

I strode back up the path wondering what to do next. I was certain the Queen was in that house. Was the Duchess hiding the Queen for the King?

As I walked, Vidocq appeared beside me.

"Where did you go?" I asked him.

"Nowhere. But I did not want to be taken into that house where I might be caged up or something."

"Good point." I sat down on a tree stump to the left of the path and looked back at the house. "I know they're hiding something. I need to shrink down and get inside there."

"*Ma petite,* you must be cautious of the shrinking and the growing too often. I cannot say for certain, but the confines of Literatia or this altered version of *Alice's Adventures in Wonderland* might make changing more volatile for you than it was for Alice."

"That may be true, but I have to sneak into that cottage to see if the Queen is there. We don't know if the Duchess killed the Queen or not, but—like the King—the Duchess might want people to believe the Queen is still alive. She could be hoping to *rule* by pretending to express the Queen's wishes or commands to the King." I took the remainder of the mushroom from my pocket.

"I wish you wouldn't," Vidocq said. "I have a bad feeling about this."

"I've taken your objection under advisement, and you have my permission to say *I told you so* if anything goes wrong." I nibbled a bit of the mushroom and immediately shrank to the size of an ant. "Oh!"

"I told you so," Vidocq said.

Turning the mushroom around, I started to take a bite off the other side.

"Wait," he said. "While you're this size, you can crawl onto my neck and hide in my fur. Duchess believes me to be her cat, so no one will be suspicious when they see me in the house. We can search for the Queen to our hearts' content. And if anyone attempts to restrain Vidocq, I'll simply disappear."

"That's a good idea."

Vidocq eased along side the stump where I was now standing, and I reached out to take hold of his fur. As I did so, I grew to an inch tall.

"*Pourquoi?* Why did you bite the mushroom? Did you not just agree that Vidocq had an excellent plan?"

"I didn't bite the mushroom."

He stepped back away from the stump. "Perhaps you should not climb onto Vidocq's neck, *n'est-ce pas?* What if you suddenly grow to be ten feet tall and crush Vidocq like the bug?"

I sighed. "Okay. I'll find a way inside and—"

"You may hold to my tail and hide behind me as I stroll into the house," he said. "But let go immediately should you feel a growth explosion coming on, *s'il te plait.* Once again, I told you so."

As he was speaking, I shrank down to half an inch

tall. I gulped. The pit in my stomach was telling me I'd made a grave mistake.

"We must solve this mystery post haste and get you out of this manuscript as soon as possible. I fear your molecular structure has become unstable."

Reader, I'm not sure how Vidocq's feline face was able to look so concerned, but he managed to pull it off. His face probably mirrored my own terror.

I half expected him to tell me everything would be all right, but we knew each other too well for that. We wouldn't lie to each other. He was right. The best thing I could do was find out who killed the Queen as quickly as possible, have the manuscript reset, and get out of the world of this book.

We started back down the path; but because I was so small, I could only take tiny steps. It seemed to take forever for us to get a distance that would have normally taken us a few seconds. In fact, Vidocq lay down on the path and waited for me.

Striding back in my direction, he said, "This is taking too long. The book will be destroyed before you even make it to the cottage at this rate." He picked me up in his teeth.

I glanced down and realized how very far from the ground I was. I hoped the material of my dress was stronger than I'd imagined.

Squeezing my eyes shut, I felt the cool wind in my face as Vidocq sprinted to the cottage. I didn't open my eyes again until he'd placed me back onto the ground.

"I see an open window," he said. He grasped me by the back of my collar again and leapt onto the windowsill. He let me go. "Shall we split up or stay together?"

"Stay with me please," I said. "I have no idea what might happen next."

CHAPTER 6

Once Vidocq and I were in the house, he began to fade.

"What are you doing?" I hissed, although as small as I was, I doubt the Duchess or the Cook would have heard me had I shouted.

"I am turning invisible in order to search the rooms more efficiently."

At this point, only his head was visible.

"I thought you were going to stay with me."

Reader, I'm not proud of the fact that I sounded like a petulant child, but I was scared!

"If we are to find the Queen, I cannot. It would take hours for you to simply walk across the room the size you are currently."

"But aren't you afraid you won't be able to make yourself visible again?" I rubbed my forehead. "I mean, my eating the mushrooms have caused my size to become unstable. What if the same thing happens to you?"

"It won't, *ma chere*," he said. "The Cheshire cat always had the innate ability to fade in and out. Alice's size was manipulated by what she ate and drank. You wait here, and I'll quickly search the house for the Queen."

"All right." Frowning, I looked around at all the gigantic things littering the floor. A length of thread that looked like a blue rope to me, a thimble as tall as I was that had fallen onto its side, a needle that—to me—was as large as a javelin. Apparently, this was a sewing room.

"Don't be frightened," he said. "I'll be back soon. Just stay under something and out of the way of feet."

I gasped. Vidocq was right—I could be trampled to death and still go completely unnoticed by my killer. I hurried to hide behind the leg of the sewing table and prayed that Vidocq would return soon. Being so small was terrifying. I had a new respect for ants.

From my hiding place, I strained my ears to hear Vidocq's paws on the hardwood floor, but I couldn't. Either he had a delicate step—after all, he *was* a cat—or else, he'd already left the room.

Within moments, I heard a clicking sound. Rather than coming from the direction of the door to the sewing room, however, it was coming from behind me. The chill that tickled the back of my neck warned me that this was definitely not Vidocq I heard.

I whirled around.

Facing me was a silverfish. It would have been icky

had I been my normal size, but this one was nearly as long as I was tall. The two antennae on its head were reaching out toward me, waving like one of those inflatable tube things you might see in front of a car dealership.

"You were warned," it said, its voice sounding scratchy and dry.

"I'm not afraid of you."

Reader, that was a bald-faced lie. Or maybe not, if you consider that afraid *wasn't a strong enough word for what I was feeling.*

"So many of us wanting to destroy you, and it's going to be me. What accolades will be heaped upon me!"

It came closer, rearing up on two of its legs and reaching for me with the other four. I ducked behind the thimble and, not taking my eyes off the silverfish, felt around for the needle. I felt the cold steel rod beneath my palm and lifted it.

"Stay back!" I warned. "I don't want to hurt you, but I will."

"There is where we differ, tiny human. I *do* want to hurt you, and I have every intention of doing so."

The silverfish advanced on me, and I brought my other hand up to get a better grip on the needle. I jabbed it in the creature's direction, but it was quicker than I was and avoided being stabbed.

It was a scaly, silvery blur as it moved, and I felt its prickly legs snake around my waist.

Screaming, I stabbed at one of the legs with the

needle, until the silverfish let me go. I turned to face it again, but it had run around and was behind me again. I spun around, jabbing the needle blindly, hoping to hit the silverfish or to at least make it keep its distance, but it was hard to fight an enemy that was so much faster than I.

I felt two of its legs wrap around my arm. It was my right arm—my right hand was holding the needle—and the insect was tightening its grip so that I was unable to transfer the needle to my other hand. In fact, my arm was tingling. I was trying to wrench that arm away from the silverfish while trying to fight it off with the rest of my body hitting, kicking, and thrashing, but I wasn't making any progress.

Realizing my efforts were merely tiring me out, I decided to be still. If the nasty beast thought it had won, maybe I could catch it off guard and get away.

As soon as I stopped moving, the silverfish laughed. Although that sound was sickening, the roar I heard following that laughter evoked memories of watching nature documentaries with my cousins when we were young. I prayed the growling was coming from Vidocq and not from some other creature that I was going to have to try and fight.

The silverfish's legs were pried off my arm by some unseen claws or fangs. I wanted to spear the silverfish with my makeshift sword, but since I couldn't see Vidocq, I thought it best to let him handle the situation from here.

The last I saw of the silverfish, it was being slung out the window.

"Thank you," I said. "If I could see your head, I would kiss you."

"I will claim my kiss *a bientot*—soon. I have found the Queen's body in a bedroom and will take you there."

He picked me up in his teeth and bounded to the room where the Queen was lying on the bed.

"Could you please get me up there onto the bed?" I asked.

Vidocq leapt up onto the bed and placed me on the blanket that was covering the Queen.

I was close to the Queen's head, and as I leaned forward to examine it, I felt myself grow larger and hit my head on the ceiling. "Ouch!"

Dropping to my knees, I asked Vidocq, "Where are you?"

His twitching tail emerged on the other side of the bed.

"Look at this." I pointed to the jagged edges around the Queen's neck. "It appears her head was torn off rather than cut with any precision."

"Do you now believe the Queen's death to have been an accident?" he asked.

"No. I think the Queen was killed by someone or something larger than a playing card."

"Maybe so, but don't forget the King is a silverfish and could have gotten a group of them to do his bidding. And cards, like books, are made of paper, *ma petite*. They are certainly not a delicacy like ancient manuscripts, but they are edible."

"What are you doing, you horrible girl?"

I whipped my head around to see the Duchess rushing toward the bed. I hurriedly got up, leaving the bed between us.

"How dare you disturb my sister while she's sleeping!"

"Duchess, the Queen isn't sleeping," I said. "She's dead."

"Oh, that's rot and nonsense!" The Duchess's face was getting redder by the second. "You'd better be glad my sister is a heavy sleeper, or else she'd have your head chopped off for your insolence."

"It isn't insolence. If you don't believe me, try and wake her."

"I'll do no such thing," the Duchess said. "I won't have the Queen angry with *me* for disturbing her rest. The Queen is very busy and has a lot of responsibilities. I try to help her whenever I can."

"Like now?" I asked.

"Of course. Where else but here could the Queen find rest and rejuvenation away from the palace and all of the kingdom's demands?"

"Did you bring the Queen here from the meadow?"

The Duchess hesitated, seemingly weighing whether she wanted to tell me or not. Finally, she said, "Cook was out gathering mushrooms for the soup when she came upon the Queen fast asleep. She came back to the cottage and reported her discovery to me. We returned together and brought the Queen back here to finish her nap."

"I'm sure that if you'll take a closer look, you'll see that the Queen isn't sleeping." I gestured to the Queen's head, which was not attached to her body.

Reader, I hope you aren't freaked out by my apparent insensitivity. I wouldn't have been so calm had there been a bloody head in the bed next to the Queen's body, but with her being a playing card, it was surreal...and not bloody in the slightest. Plus, I was getting frustrated with everyone telling me that I wasn't seeing what I was seeing.

"Oh, you ignorant girl!" The Duchess flailed her arms. "The Queen has lost her head! What of it? Doesn't everyone lose his or her head at some time or another? Besides, the Queen's head isn't *lost*—it's right there!" As the Duchess yelled at me, her grotesque facial features reddened to the consistency of a ripe beefsteak tomato.

The Cook stuck her head around the doorframe keeping herself well away from the Duchess's wrath. "Two more girls are here to see you, Duchess."

"What two girls? Are they like *her*?"

Rather than answer the Duchess's question, Cook simply ducked her head out of the room and sent the two girls inside.

I recognized them immediately. They were Alice's sisters, Lorina and Edith. What were they doing here? *How* were they here? They weren't characters in *Alice's Adventures Under Ground* or *Alice's Adventures in Wonderland*—were they?

Upon seeing Lorina and Edith, the Duchess smiled broadly and opened her arms. "What a delightful surprise! I didn't expect to see either of you today."

Lorina suffered through the Duchess's embrace, but Edith hugged the Duchess as if they were best friends.

"We're here for Alice," Edith said.

"Yes, Alice," Lorina said softly. "Mother is going to be angry if you don't come home at once."

"I'll be there soon," I said. "I have to find something first."

"Whatever it is you've lost, it will still be lost tomorrow." Edith smiled, and I nearly gasped when I saw a silverfish slither across her teeth. "Come back and find it then."

Feeling a sudden pressure on my shoulder, I stiffened.

"Shhh, it's me," Vidocq whispered. "You mustn't go with them."

I turned my back to my audience so they wouldn't see me whispering to the invisible cat. "What can I do?"

"We'll think of something, *ma petite*. Vidocq will help."

The Duchess came over to me and began examining the floor in front of where I was standing. "What is it you're looking for?"

"It's...um...not a thing." I struggled for an explanation. "I'm searching for the King. I want to let him know the Queen has been found."

"Oh, is that all?" She patted my arm. "Don't fret about that for a moment, dear. I will send a message to the King that all is well."

"That worked out beautifully," I mumbled.

"Indeed, it did!" The Duchess beamed. "And now you may go home to dinner."

Lorina stepped over to me and took my hand. "You're a dear girl to always be so concerned with everyone else. Allow me to take care of *you*."

I peered at her face. Was she a silverfish like Edith? What were they planning to do to me?

Smiling, Lorina said, "Don't be so worried, silly. Mother isn't *that* angry."

There was no sign of a silverfish in her smile.

"I still don't know what to do." I was speaking to Vidocq and knew he'd recognize that fact, but Lorina thought I was talking to her.

"You'll go home and have dinner with your family, and you'll let the Duchess care for her sister," she said.

"Okay." I allowed Lorina to lead me from the Duchess's house. As we stepped over the threshold, I shrank to about an inch high and found myself in a dark, wet cave.

CHAPTER 7

It wasn't until he spit me out that I realized the cave I'd been in was Vidocq's mouth. Those stalagmites and stalactites had been feline teeth.

He materialized as I sat on the ground wiping my face on a flower petal that I'd found on the ground beside me. "Before you fuss at Vidocq, you should realize I was taking my life in my hands scooping you into my mouth like that. Had you grown big again, you would have broken my jaw."

"I appreciate your quick thinking."

"Yes, well, sorry for the bath." He plucked a daisy and dropped it at my feet so I could finish drying off.

"Thank you." Using both hands, I tugged a white petal from the daisy. "He loves me?" I laughed.

"*Oui*. Whether you speak of Vidocq or Matthew or someone else entirely, the answer is always *oui*."

"Flatterer." Using the petal, I dried my damp hair. "I'm

confused about Alice's sisters. How are they even here? And how is one a silverfish while the other—as far as I could see—is not?"

Vidocq stretched out on the ground beside me. "You will recall, *ma petite*, that Alice was sitting with her older sister on the riverbank at the beginning of the story. That would be Lorina."

"But Edith wasn't in the story."

"No, but then this Edith isn't Edith, is she?" he asked.

"Good point. Still, how could the silverfish even know about her if she isn't in the original manuscript?"

"*Monsieur* Carroll wrote *Alice's Adventures Under Ground* to entertain Alice and her sisters during a boating trip. That's a fact the silverfish would be aware of. To use both Alice's older and younger sisters to do their bidding is a nice touch."

"Lorina seemed to truly care about Alice and want to get her home," I said. "What was Edith up to?"

"I would imagine she, too, wanted Alice to go home. If Alice—*you*—leave the story, then the mystery remains unsolved, and the silverfish may do whatever they like."

"And that will ultimately destroy the manuscript."

"*Oui.*"

An image in a droplet of water clinging to the daisy petal on my lap caught my attention. The scene was moving, and I bent closer to figure out what was going on.

There was a handsome young man wearing fawn-colored breeches, black boots, and a navy tailcoat. He was dancing with a woman wearing an emerald green ballgown. Her back was to me, so I couldn't see her face. They danced with such grace, and it was obvious they were in love. He was holding her close, and her gloved hand caressed his face. He said something to her, and she threw back her head and laughed.

"*C'est moi.* It's me."

"It is!" I laughed. "Oh, Vidocq, look how handsome you are. And is this your wife? Or simply one of your many conquests?"

The couple turned, and I could see the woman's face. She looked like me. Not me as Alice—but me, Gia. I squinted at the drop of water. "Is that—?"

"It's you." His voice was barely a whisper.

"We're having a wonderful time," I said. "I wonder what book we're in?"

A beautiful black and orange monarch butterfly landed in front of us. "You can be in any book you want, my dear. This particular scene is from an early, unpublished Jane Austen work."

The Butterfly was quiet for a moment as Vidocq and I watched a version of ourselves waltzing in a ballroom among other couples yet still seemingly in our own little world.

"Drink it in," the Butterfly said, its voice barely above a whisper. "Your happiness, your love…. The two of you could even have children."

I knew Vidocq had no children, and I glanced at his face. He was looking wistful.

"Imagine the life you could have. It would be a fairy-tale." The Butterfly's voice was lilting. Mesmerizing.

"Until the silverfish destroy the manuscript," I said, tearing my eyes away from the scene and glaring at the Butterfly.

"They won't. The Council sent me to give you their word. They want to make peace with you...to allow the two of you to live in peace and harmony forever."

"But it's a lie—it's make-believe." I looked to Vidocq for help, but he was still staring at the scene playing out within the drop of water.

"It doesn't have to be a lie for you," the Butterfly said.

"I'm in love with Matthew."

Reader, that butterfly knew just how to come at me.

"Matthew is happy at home with his son at last. Why, after you sacrificed so much to get him there would you want to drag him away? Now *you* are trapped in Litera-tia. Would you want him to grow old waiting for you?"

My mouth had gone dry. Was I trapped here indefinitely? Matthew had been trapped for decades and had missed much of his son's life. The two of us might never be together.

Vidocq was also trapped in Literatia. Sure, he could move from book to book; but to the real world, he'd died in 1857.

The Butterfly turned its attention to Vidocq, whose feline eyes had filled with tears. "Are you not tired of being a nomad, *mon ami*? Even during your natural life, you never settled down. Wouldn't you like to do so now?

To have the love of a beautiful young woman—your wife? To have children to adore and nurture?"

Vidocq nodded, and a tear rolled down his furry cheek.

"Oh, Vidocq!" I leaned over and laid my head against his paw.

My movement disturbed the water droplet, and the image disappeared. Still, the feelings it had stirred up didn't evaporate. The Butterfly's suggestion was so sweet and seductive.

If I truly loved Matthew, I'd want him to be happy and with his son, wouldn't I? Maybe I could bargain with the silverfish somehow to make them leave the wonderful old manuscripts alone. Then Matthew and Cooper wouldn't have to come to Literatia anymore. They'd never have to put themselves in danger again.

"You'd both be so happy," the Butterfly continued quietly. "You'd have everything you could possibly want."

"I'd want to know that Matthew and Cooper were all right," I said. "What if I became a writer in the new book —a virtual Austen—who could quickly produce manu-scripts that the silverfish could feast on?"

"What a delightful idea!" The Butterfly smiled.

"And they'd stop eating the classics?" I asked. "Would they honestly go for that?"

"I'll check with them and see. But, in the meantime, let us go to your new world. I can take us all there now."

I sat up in order to look at Vidocq's face. "What do you think of all this?"

Before he could answer, something swooped down, grabbed me by the shoulders, and carried me up into the sky.

Unable to tell if I was as far from the ground as I believed I was, or if it merely looked that way because I was so small, I screamed as if my life was over. I imagined it probably was.

I should have jumped at the deal the Butterfly offered. Now this whatever-it-was was going to drop me and kill me, and I was going to be dead both in Literatia and in the real world. Matthew probably wouldn't even know what had happened to me. He might not even care! After all, in that other drop of water I saw, he was kissing someone else.

The creature landed among the top branches of a large tree and sat me down on a thick bough. Trembling, I turned to see that my captor was the Gryphon.

I stared at him open-mouthed and drew in a shuddering breath.

"You're welcome," he said.

Wrapping my arms around myself, I asked, "What?"

"You are welcome."

"For what?" I asked. "You just scared the Dickens out of me."

"Well, I hope not." He smiled, inasmuch as someone with a beak could smile. "We might have to visit another of his works sometime."

"I'm so frightened and confused."

"I know, sweetheart, but I'm here now."

"*Matthew?*"

He nodded.

"But, how?"

Before he could answer, I grew again and nearly fell out of the tree.

"Careful," he said.

"My size is out of whack, and I can't control it." I hugged him. "Thank goodness you're here. Is that selfish of me to say?"

"No. Why would you think it would be? What was the Butterfly saying to you?"

"The Butterfly made me realize it would be horrible of me to keep you and Cooper apart, especially now that I'm trapped here in Literatia," I said. "It told Vidocq and me that it could provide a fairytale world for us, with the permission of the Council of the Silverfish."

"And you believed that?"

"I saw you kissing someone else. I thought you'd abandoned me."

"Gia." He tsked. "You know better than to believe everything you see and hear in Literatia, especially in a story so fraught with symbolism and fantasy. You're looking for the murderer of a playing card, for crying out loud."

"I know, but—"

He wrapped his paws and wings around me, and I nestled against his warmth and security.

"The Butterfly is a liar. It will say anything it has to in

order to deceive you. The silverfish would never willingly grant you a happily-ever-after."

"It was just so pretty and convincing," I said.

"So, I've heard, was Lucifer."

I buried my face in his fur. "What about Vidocq? We left him alone with the Butterfly."

"He'll be all right," Matthew said. "He won't go anywhere without you, and the Butterfly won't feel the need to try to convince him further without you there. Once the creature leaves Vidocq alone, he'll realize that the Butterfly was trying to sell you both a pack of lies."

"I hope so. Vidocq was so sad."

"The Butterfly is a master manipulator." Matthew released me so I could get a better look at him. He spread his wings. "What do you think?"

"Impressive." I grinned. "Almost as impressive as you were as Edward Rochester."

"Almost? Wow." He chuckled before turning serious again. "Are you all right physically? Other than not being able to maintain a size?"

"I'm okay. This place is just… a lot. I mean, I thought the worlds of *Jane Eyre* and *A Tale of Two Cities* were overwhelming, but *this*." I shook my head. "Nothing is what it seems." A thought occurred to me. "How can I be sure you *are* Matthew?"

"I thought you could usually tell from my eyes," he said.

"Usually, but again, in Wonderland, nothing is what it appears to be."

"When you first arrived, you had a letter from me in your pocket. I told you that your wedding ring was safe in North Carolina. What I didn't tell you is that it's in the silver, heart-shaped box on the mantel."

Only someone who'd been in the library would know about that box. Laughing, I threw my arms around him. "It *is* you!"

"It is."

I drew back. "What now? How do we get out of here?"

"I'm afraid that question isn't so easily answered."

CHAPTER 8

Matthew, or rather the Gryphon (to avoid confusion), left me in the tree to go find Vidocq. I'd been afraid the Butterfly might find me while I was in the tree alone, but the Gryphon reminded me that I was larger than the Butterfly now. Therefore, I sat and waited and hoped I didn't shrink again.

Reader, I would be delighted to get out of Wonderland. This place was some kind of psychedelic nightmare.

Running my hands along the rough bark beneath me, I leaned against the trunk of the tree, and inhaled deeply. The scent of pine was soothing, and I rested my head against the tree trunk.

I glanced down, realized how far away the ground was, and decided to keep my eyes facing forward.

A red squirrel poked its head out of a knothole. "Who are you, and what are you doing here?"

"You may call me Alice, and I'm here because the Gryphon flew me up here."

"I'm sorry for your misfortune," the Squirrel said. "I'm terrified of the Gryphon. I would help you hide, if I could, but you are too big to fit into my home."

"I am now," I said. "Give it a minute."

"What's that?"

"Nothing. Tell me why you're afraid of the Gryphon."

"Everyone knows the Gryphon works for the Queen," the Squirrel said. "He must have brought you up here and left you to die."

"No, he went to find our friend," I said. "The Gryphon —*this* Gryphon—doesn't work for the Queen. He's—"

"The Gryphon works for the Queen," the Squirrel repeated. "Everyone knows that. I am truly sorry for your misfortune."

With that, the Squirrel turned and scampered into the knothole.

I wanted to call out to the Squirrel that the Queen was dead, and that even if she wasn't, the Gryphon wasn't under her control, but I guessed I'd have been wasting my breath.

The Gryphon *wasn't* under the Queen's control. He wasn't under anyone's control except his own. Because he wasn't the Gryphon at all. He was Matthew. Right?

Nothing in Wonderland is as it seems.

What if the Gryphon wasn't Matthew after all? What if I was being deceived again? I searched for a way out of the tree, but I couldn't find one.

66

"Squirrel!" I called. "Please help me! Can you tell me how to get down from here?"

"You could climb or fall." Its voice came from deep within the tree. "I don't think you would survive either way."

"Gee, thanks!"

"You're welcome!"

Before I could figure out a way down, the Gryphon returned, clamped its talons onto my shoulders, and flew me down to the ground where Vidocq was waiting.

"Poor Vidocq." I went to him and sat on the ground beside him. "You don't appear to be your fun-loving self. I'm sorry the Butterfly upset you."

"It is nothing. The Gryphon found me and informed me that he had taken you to safety." He raised his head as imperiously as a real cat. "He knew I could take care of myself. As soon as the Gryphon snatched you up and flew away, I ran after you; but I failed to keep up with the powerful Gryphon."

"The Gryphon told me the Butterfly was trying to deceive us."

"*Oui*, I know. I should have slapped the wretched insect so hard it would have been grinning at the daisy roots."

"It would what?" I asked.

"Be dead and buried," the Gryphon said.

"Oh." I nodded. "Still the Butterfly sure did paint an intriguing picture."

"That it did. It could almost make me imagine I could

recapture my youth, make up for past regrets, and live a life of pure bliss."

Gently resting a hand on Vidocq's back, I said, "And it nearly convinced me that we could live a life free from worry and hardship--that I could simply pen master-pieces that the silverfish would dine on and that none of us would have to risk our lives to fight them again."

"Even if the Butterfly made good on any of its promises, which is highly unlikely, we'd have all been bored senseless," the Gryphon said. "Now, bring me up to speed on the murder investigation."

Whether this Gryphon was Matthew or not, I felt as if I didn't have a choice but to trust him at this point. I'd seen no silverfish in his mouth when he'd attempted to smile, but did that count since he had no teeth?

"Our two primary suspects are the Duchess and the King," I said. "Both have much more control—or in the Duchess's case, the potential of control--with the Queen out of the way. I also found the Dormouse suspicious."

"Why's that?" The Gryphon paced in front of Vidocq and me.

"She kept insisting that the Queen's death was an accident." I shook my head. "On the other hand, she's awfully tiny. I don't see how she could have ripped the head off the Queen."

"A mushroom or some other concoction could turn a tiny mouse into an enormous mouse for long enough to commit a murder," Vidocq said.

"I hadn't even considered the possibility that other

characters would use mushrooms or the 'drink me' and 'eat me' morsels to grow and shrink," I said. "Alice was the only one to do so in the original manuscript. But, of course, any of the characters could."

The Gryphon stilled. "I hear something."

Despite my heartbeat in my ears, I heard something too. It was a man's voice. Singing.

Vidocq sprang to his feet, and both he and the Gryphon took defensive stances. Not wanting to be the proverbial sitting duck, I rose as well.

The Hatter wandered into the clearing. "Hello, hello." He wagged a finger at Alice. "You ran off without your tea."

"Um...my apologies," I said.

"Accepted! You may come back and have your tea now."

"May my friends come also?"

He tapped his chin with his forefinger as he eyed both the Gryphon and the Cheshire Cat with suspicion. "I don't know how my companions would feel about having an eagle-lion thingy and a cat joining us for tea."

"We promise not to hurt your friends," the Gryphon said.

"Pinkie pie, finger in the eye?" the Hatter asked.

It was nonsense, but both the Gryphon and Vidocq dutifully repeated the Hatter's words.

"Very well then! Come along!" The Hatter began to lead the way. "The March Hare was terribly disappointed when you left, miss. I tried to explain to him that you were off to find the Queen."

"Actually, I was searching for the King" I said.

"The King, you say? I had no idea he was lost. Did you find him?"

"I did."

"Good. That takes care of that then. Now we may enjoy our tea."

"Mr. Hatter, have you ever eaten anything that made you grow smaller or larger?" I asked.

He laughed. "How utterly ridiculous. Why would I ever do a silly thing like that?"

"Perhaps it would be convenient to be a different size sometimes." I gestured toward Vidocq. "Just as the Cheshire Cat sometimes finds it helpful to be invisible."

"Oh, I've pulled that trick a time or two," the Hatter said. "In fact, I'm invisible from the tea party right this very instant."

"You are absent from the tea party, sir." I hoped he wouldn't be vexed by my correcting him. "You aren't invisible."

"The other members of the tea party cannot see me; therefore, I am most assuredly invisible."

I gave up. "Is the Dormouse still at the party?"

"I imagine she is—unless she has turned invisible. Why?"

"She didn't seem to like me," I said. "Perhaps she won't be pleased that you've brought me back."

The Hatter sighed. "The Dormouse truly is an argumentative soul, and she can be quite ferocious. It's better not to provoke her."

"Did I provoke her earlier?" I asked.

"You must have done," the Hatter said.

"How? What did I do?"

Before the Hatter could hazard a guess—had he been going to give me an answer—I shrank.

He looked around. "Where did she go? Did she turn invisible?"

"No!" I shouted. "I'm down here!" I waved my arms, but the Hatter didn't look down. Neither did Vidocq or the Gryphon. "Anybody?"

Wanting to avoid being stomped on at all costs, I grabbed hold of the fur on the Gryphon's hind paw and pulled myself up. I still wasn't a hundred percent certain he was Matthew, but I knew that perching on his foot would keep me from being trampled.

The Gryphon flicked his tail around. "Hold tight."

Vidocq, hearing the Gryphon's instructions, looked down and spotted me. "Ah, look! Alice is here, Mr. Hatter. She's smaller, but she is here."

"You are trying to trick me," he said. "Alice turned invisible so she could run ahead of us to the tea party. I find that inexcusably rude, and I no longer want to have tea with her." He gave a slight bow. "If you'll excuse me, gentlemen, I'm going home. Good day."

"He could've seen me had he only looked," I said. When I got no response, I shouted, "Do we want to go on to the tea party?"

"If you believe the Dormouse to be the killer, then we should go there," Vidocq said. "It is imperative that we find the Queen's killer as soon as possible."

"I'd like to see the Queen for myself before we go to the tea party," the Gryphon said.

"Why? What could you discover that we have not? Gia must leave the book immediately. You and I can find the murderer and reset the book ourselves, Matthew."

"While it's true that we might be able to determine who killed the Queen, the character of Alice is crucial to the book," the Gryphon said. "It can't continue without her in it. If Gia leaves, the Alice who would be left in her place might be so changed by the silverfishes' destruction that she would be no help to us at all. She might even be a detriment."

"I agree," I said. "Plus, Alice never completely disappeared in the story."

"In the *original* story." Vidocq huffed. "This is no longer the original story."

"Okay." I took hold of the Gryphon's tail. "We'll solve the murder as quickly as we possibly can, and then we can all escape this book. Let's head to the Duchess's house to allow the Gryphon to see the Queen. Maybe his eagle eyes will see some clue we overlooked."

CHAPTER 9

At the Duchess's house, Vidocq led us around the house to the room where the Queen's body was being kept. The window was open slightly.

Leaping onto the windowsill, Vidocq attempted to raise the window further with his paws. "It's stuck."

"Allow me." The Gryphon put his talons onto the window as I wrapped his tail around my fist to keep from falling off his foot.

When the Gryphon couldn't get the window open either, I tugged on his tail to get his attention. He lowered one talon, and I abandoned the paw so he could lift me close to his face.

"Put me on the windowsill," I said. "I can go inside, see what's jamming the window, and we can try to fix it to allow Vidocq to get in and for you to at least put your head into the room and get a better look."

"That sounds like a solid plan." He placed me on the windowsill.

I quickly slipped under the raised window and scrambled onto the other side of the sill. I was looking up to see what was keeping the window from not moving as it should when—you guessed it—I grew to be about a foot tall and fell from the casement.

Giving a startled cry as I fell backward, I landed on the bed next to the Queen's severed head, a situation that would have been truly disgusting had I still been in the world of *A Tale of Two Cities*.

Me and my big mouth, Reader. I might as well have yelled, "Come and get me!"

The Duchess, the Cook, Lorina, and Edith hurried into the room.

"Oh, what a relief!" Lorina scooped me up in a hug. "We must get you and your sister home right away."

"Of course, you must," the Duchess said. "This mischievous girl has been creating an uproar all day long. First large, then small, now somewhere in between. I say one should be what one seems to be. Never mind how determined she is to keep the Queen from resting."

"I can't control my size," I said. "Earlier, I ate a pinch off a mushroom to make myself grow smaller and then again to grow taller. Now, I'm not doing anything but am still growing and shrinking willy-nilly."

"You're tired, dear," Lorina said. "As Mr. Dodgson once said, 'All in the golden afternoon full leisurely we glide, for both our oars, with little skill, by little arms are plied, while little hands make vain pretense our wanderings to guide.'"

I recognized the quote as the first stanza of the poem from the preface of *Alice's Adventures in Wonderland*.

"Yes!" Edith enthusiastically recited the end of the poem. "'And now the tale is done, and home we steer'— she added emphasis to the word *home*— "'A merry crew, beneath the setting sun. Alice! A childish story take, and with a gentle hand, lay it where Childhood's dreams are twined in Memory's mystic band, like pilgrim's withered wreath of flowers plucked in a far-off land.'"

"That's right, Edith," Lorina said. "We've had a delightful visit to Wonderland, but it's time that little girls like you and Alice go home, have their dinner, and then cuddle up to their big sister by the fire and tell her of their adventures."

Vidocq sprang from the doorway and onto the bed.

"It's that cat!" Edith shouted. "He's the one who helped her escape last time. Somebody catch him and hold him."

The Duchess tutted and shook her head. "He always has been a mischievous cat, creating an uproar all day long. First appearing, then disappearing—one never knows where he might show up next."

As Edith, the Duchess, and the Cook began trying to catch Vidocq, he disappeared. The trio bumped into each other time and time again as they struggled to catch something other than thin air.

Lorina calmly took my hand and led me out of the room.

"What about Edith?" I asked.

"She'll be fine. I imagine we'll see her again later." She smiled down at me. "Edith isn't really like you and me, is she?"

I wondered if Lorina knew Edith was a silverfish. "What do you mean?"

Shrugging, she said, "Edith is still very young. She has a lot of her childhood left. You're growing up quickly, Alice, and so am I. I'll be expected to marry and have a family of my own soon." She squeezed my hand. "I wish I could protect you from all of life's hardships."

Alice Liddell had suffered many hardships in her adult life. She was widowed and lost two sons in World War I, and she became destitute and had to sell the original manuscript given to her by Charles Dodgson. Did Lorina somehow know all this? Or was she speaking generally? Maybe she was afraid of the hardships she herself might face when she left her parents' home.

"If only we could remain as young and carefree as we are right now, Alice," she said. "Wouldn't that be wonderful?"

"It would," I said, even though I was a far cry from *carefree* at the moment.

I heard something behind us and turned to see Vidocq materialize and then make himself invisible again before Lorina could see him. I gave him a slight nod.

"Lorina, would you please wait for me here while I go and see the King? I'll hurry, I promise."

"Why on earth would you want to see the King?" she asked.

"He needs to know that the Queen is with the Duchess."

Shaking her head, Lorina said, "We'll send him a message."

"You know we won't. Once we leave Wonderland, there will be no turning back," I said.

"Is that so bad?"

"No...not so long as I've done my best not to leave any unfinished business behind. I went to find the King and brought him to where I'd found the Queen earlier today, but she wasn't there anymore. It was before I knew the Duchess and the Cook had taken her home." I rubbed my forehead. "He accused me of being a cruel prankster, and I want to prove to him that I'm not."

"Alice, dear, the King's opinion is of no consequence to us," she said.

"I know, but it's important to me. Please stay here and wait for me. I'll come back as soon as I can."

Lorina continued to protest. "Our supper will be cold, and Mother will be cross."

"I can go very quickly," I said.

"How?"

"My friends will ensure that my visit with the King is expeditious."

Before Lorina could raise any more objections, the

Gryphon swooped in, took me by the shoulders, and flew away with me. I could hear Lorina shouting.

"I hate to scare her like that," I said.

"She'll be fine." He landed and placed me on the ground a short enough distance away that Vidocq would be able to find us easily. "What do you intend to do next?"

"I told Lorina the truth—to an extent. I'm going back to the castle and tell the King that I've located the Queen at the Duchess's house. I believe there's a good chance that he killed the Queen to usurp her power." I spread my hands. "You know how they were in the original manuscript. The Queen blustered around telling everyone she was going to have them executed while the King quietly told the soldiers to ignore her orders. With the Queen dead, he has no opposition in running the kingdom as he pleases."

Vidocq approached as I was explaining my position to the Gryphon. "What it is you intend to do, *ma petite*? Are you going to simply accuse the King of killing the Queen?"

"No. I'm going to tell him I've found her resting at the Duchess's house and that the Duchess and the Cook took her there from the field where I originally found her," I said. "I'm hoping that when the King goes there and sees the Queen, I can get him to acknowledge that she's not resting but is, in fact, dead."

"How will that help?" Vidocq asked.

"If they acknowledge that the Queen is dead, then the

Duchess and the King will likely begin to accuse each other of killing her, and one of them will end up confessing under the pressure." I smiled.

Neither Vidocq nor the Gryphon—as far as I could tell—smiled back.

"I think it will not work." Vidocq slowly shook his head.

"What about Lorina?" the Gryphon asked. "Why do you have her waiting for you at the edge of the forest near the Duchess's house?"

"I didn't want to just abandon her," I said. "I believe she truly cares about Alice. Once we have the confession of the murderer, the book should reset, and Alice will awake beside Lorina on the riverbank."

"I hope you know what you're doing," the Gryphon said.

"So do I."

We had only taken a few steps when I heard a deep, languid voice say, "I can make it stop, you know."

I stopped. "Did you hear that?" I looked around until I spotted smoke.

"I heard," Vidocq said. "It's that infernal caterpillar. He can't be trusted."

"No one in Wonderland can be trusted," the Gryphon said, "especially not since the silverfish have corrupted it."

Walking closer to the rising plume of smoke, I discovered the Caterpillar. He was sitting on a rock, smoking his hookah and looking bored.

"What do you mean, you can make it stop?" I asked.

"Your size fluctuations."

"I don't believe you." Vidocq loomed over the Caterpillar.

If it was his intention to intimidate the creature, he was disappointed.

"Believe whatever you'd like," the Caterpillar said. "It makes no difference to me."

"How?" I asked.

He decided to be obtuse. "How what?"

"How can you make me stop growing or shrinking without warning?"

Taking a puff from his hookah, he gazed at me indifferently. He blew out the smoke and took another drag before answering. "Do you still have any of the mushroom you picked following our first meeting?"

"Yes." I patted my left pocket to make sure the mushroom morsel was still there.

"Put the entire piece into your mouth and swallow it whole," he said.

Eyes wide, I looked at the Gryphon, who shook his head.

"Don't do it, *ma petite*." Vidocq flattened his ears. "It's a trick."

"Again, *mes amis*, I couldn't care less if young Alice grows and shrinks with every breath she takes." The Caterpillar shrugged. "In fact, I find it rather amusing."

"If you find it so amusing, then laugh." I anchored my hands on my hips as I sent this shot across the bow.

As before, he refused to be challenged. "I shall never be transparent. For reasons I can't comprehend myself, I offered you a solution to your problem. Do it. Don't do it. See if I care."

The Caterpillar slid off the rock, but the Gryphon caught him in one sharp talon. "Give me a reason not to swallow *you* whole."

Chuckling, the Caterpillar said, "Do what you will, Gryphon. Your threats are ineffective."

"Who *are* you, and what are you about?" the Gryphon asked.

"I'm simply an observer. That's all I have to say."

The Gryphon let the Caterpillar go, and the insouciant blue bug went on its way at an unhurried pace, leaving all three of us wondering what—if anything—it was up to and leaving me contemplating what would happen if I *did* swallow the rest of that mushroom.

CHAPTER 10

"Cat, would you mind scouting up ahead to intercept any other hindrances on the way to the castle?" the Gryphon asked.

"*Oui.*" Vidocq looked from the Gryphon to me. "But you need only yell to have Vidocq return at once."

"Thank you, buddy, we appreciate that." The Gryphon gave him a nod and waited until Vidocq was out of sight to address me. "You don't yet trust me, do you?"

"I want to," I said. "More than you could possibly know."

"You trust the Cat."

"Yes, but he was here when I got here."

"And that makes him less suspicious than me?"

I rubbed my eyes as I contemplated his words. "Are you telling me you don't think the Cheshire Cat is Vidocq?"

"I didn't say that. It's what *you* believe that's important."

"But I don't know what to believe. About *anything*. Everything is off kilter here. I'm a little girl trying to determine who tore the head off of a playing card, and you're asking me what I *believe*? In the most surreal circumstances and environment I've ever been in?"

"First of all, you aren't a little girl trying to determine who tore the head off a playing card. You're Gia, and you're inhabiting the character of a little girl investigating the murder of a queen. Understood?"

I nodded.

"Now, then," he continued, "was it surreal when you found yourself in the world of *Jane Eyre*? How about when you were walking down the aisle on the arm of Dr. Manette in *A Tale of Two Cities*? Were either of those circumstances imaginable to you prior to your taking the job at Smithmore Manor?"

"Of course not, Matthew, but this—" I broke off, realizing that I'd called him by name. Tears welled in my eyes. "I'm sorry."

"No need to apologize, sweetheart. I needed to reinforce to you that we're on the same side, that's all."

Hugging him, I mumbled, "Stupid squirrel."

"What's that?"

"Nothing. I just need to quit believing every creature that speaks to me."

"Trust your own council and that of Vidocq and me,"

he said. "You can be absolutely sure that we're on your side."

"I know. Thank you."

As I released the Gryphon and stepped back, Vidocq called, "May I return now?"

With a chuckle, the Gryphon said, "Yes. But did you ever really leave?"

Vidocq materialized about fifty feet away. "In a manner of speaking, I did. I wish I'd had this ability in my life as a detective—and as a criminal, for that matter. I'd have had a delightful time."

I felt more at ease as we traveled on in the direction of the castle. I didn't even change sizes as we walked along, and we'd gone far enough on our journey to need to have a rest break. I was cautiously optimistic that the portions of the mushroom that I'd previously eaten had worked their way out of my system and that I was stabilizing.

Sitting on a rock, I asked, "How much farther do you think it will be?"

"Not far," Vidocq said. "But we should have a plan before we arrive, *non?*"

Before either of us could answer him, we heard twigs snapping as something large moved through the forest. Both the Gryphon and Vidocq took a protective stance in front of me before a green dragon emerged into the clearing.

I stood and climbed onto the rock on which I'd been sitting so I could get a better look at the creature. It really was a dragon. "There aren't any dragons in *Alice's Adventures in Wonderland*."

Hearing me, the dragon bowed slightly. "I am the only one. My name is Bill."

"Bill the *Lizard*?" Vidocq asked.

"I used to be." Bill moved closer to us and sat down. "And then I ate some sort of tea cake, and I was no longer Bill the Lizard but Bill the Dragon. I very much enjoy being a dragon. No one pushes me around anymore."

"Who pushed you around before?" I asked.

"Why, *you*, for one," Bill said. "You once kicked me through the chimney of the White Rabbit's house."

"That was an accident," I said. "And I'm terribly sorry. I drank something that made me too large to fit into the house. I'd have never hurt you on purpose."

Reader, I hoped he felt the same way because he wasn't a tiny lizard now—he was enormous and could kill us all if he was of a mind to do so.

"I understand. And it didn't hurt all that much." Bill slowly blinked. "It takes a special person to admit when they've outgrown their position, as you say you did that day in the White Rabbit's house."

"And did you outgrow your position?" Vidocq asked.

"Oh, no. I grew *into* my position. I was always large in stature but not large in size. Now my size and my stature are in accord." Bill gave another of those exaggerated blinks.

"It has been wonderful seeing you, but we should get going," I said. "We're looking for the King."

"Why?" Bill asked.

"Earlier today, the King went with me to locate the Queen. But she wasn't where I'd told him she'd be, and now he believes me to be either a prankster or a liar." I spread my hands. "I've since discovered that the Duchess moved the Queen into her house, so I want to let the King know where he may find his wife."

Bill tilted his head. "Are you sure the Queen is where you left her this time?"

"I am," I said.

"There is little in this life that one can be sure of." Bill got to his feet. "What if you take the King to the Duchess's house only to find that the Queen is no longer there? The King will be livid if it appears you have tricked him a second time, and he will likely throw you into the dungeon."

"But I didn't trick him in the first place!" Realizing I was shouting at a dragon, I lowered my voice. "I had no idea the Duchess and the Cook had moved the Queen."

"Perhaps you should go to the Duchess's house and get the Queen," Bill said. "Take her to him rather than making him go to her. Then he can't dispute your word."

I ran my hands through my hair. "I need the King to know where the Queen is—where she has been."

"If you take the Queen to the castle and present her to the King, then he will know where she is," he said. "What difference does it make where she has been?"

"Bill, the Queen is dead. The Duchess insists that the Queen is only sleeping, but she is dead."

"You're absolutely certain of this?" Bill asked.

"We found her in a clearing with her head torn off," Vidocq said. "Later, in the Duchess's house, the Queen was lying on a bed and her head had not been reattached. Therefore, we are confident that she is dead."

"The King has to be made to understand that Alice had nothing to do with the Queen's death," the Gryphon said. "If we take the Queen to him, rather than vice versa, won't he believe that we killed the Queen?"

"We hoped that taking him to the Queen would force the Duchess to either confess or to give the King more information about where and how she had found the Queen," I said. For some reason, I knew not to voice my suspicions about the King. "The Duchess can corroborate my initial report of finding the Queen lying in the clearing."

"You say the Queen was already dead when you found her and that you could not revive her?" Bill asked.

"No." I frowned. "I mean, yes, she was already dead when I found her, and no, I couldn't revive her."

"Very well. As a trusted confidante of the King, I shall go with you to the Duchess's house, hear her side of the story, and then carry the Queen back to the castle."

CHAPTER 11

"How did you and the King get so close?" I asked Bill as we walked along. "I thought you worked for the White Rabbit."

"I worked for the White Rabbit when I was a lizard. He was always in a rush, pushing everyone around. When I turned into a dragon, the White Rabbit realized he could never bully me again."

I nodded. "And that's when you went to work for the King?"

"I have never worked for the King," Bill said. "He despises bullies as much as I do. The two of us are friends."

"I'm sure the King can commiserate. The Queen is the worst bully I've ever met," Vidocq said.

"She certainly was—I mean, is." Bill sized each of us up one by one. "Are any of *you* bullies?"

"Absolutely not," I said.

"I thought you were, Alice, but you have since apologized for kicking me out of the chimney."

"What if we *were* ruffians?" Vidocq asked. "What would you do about it?"

Bill snorted. "I'd kick you out of Wonderland."

"You can do that?" I raised my index finger to my chin. "The King must trust you implicitly to give you such authority."

"The King has given me no authority to banish anyone from Wonderland, although I imagine he would be happy to do so should I ask. I meant that I am physically capable of kicking you out." He looked at the Gryphon. "Maybe not *you*, Gryphon, but I could certainly punt a little girl and a smirking feline a fair distance."

Vidocq clucked his tongue. "Only a *bully* would entertain the thought of kicking a child or a helpless cat."

"There is nothing helpless about you, *mon ami*," Bill said.

"How did you know I speak French?" Vidocq asked.

Bill hesitated before saying, "By your accent, of course."

I gulped and glanced at Vidocq and the Gryphon from the corner of my eye. Could Bill be a silverfish? Does he know more about us than we'd like him to know?

Reader, none of us trusted this dragon, but now I feared he was leading us into some sort of trap.

"Tell me more about your relationship with the King," I said, eager to keep Bill talking. Maybe he'd reveal something unintentionally that would help us understand what he wanted with us. "If you weren't working at the castle after leaving the White Rabbit's employ, what did you do? Did you go into business for yourself and meet the King that way?"

"I happened to be passing by the garden one day while a few of the soldiers were trying desperately to paint white roses red. I inquired as to why they were doing such a foolish thing, and they told me they'd accidentally planted white bushes rather than the red ones the Queen desired."

"Knowing the Queen, she'd originally asked for white and then changed her mind," Vidocq said. "Had they planted red, she'd have wanted white."

"Quite right. I suggested they dig up the white bushes and replace them with red. Then should the Queen request white, they would have those as well." Bill puffed out his chest. "The soldiers were naturally frightened of me. And who could blame them? I am an imposing creature—a far cry from the lizard I used to be. Eight was particularly intimidated."

I decided to make a joke, hoping Bill would laugh or at least smile. "That reminds me of a joke. Why was Six afraid of Seven? Because Seven ate Nine!"

Bill looked down at me, his expression blank.

"Don't you get it? Seven, Eight, Nine—Seven *ate* Nine?"

"I understand the joke, but slander is never amusing. Seven is a good soldier, a friend who would never devour a comrade. Furthermore, Six is valiant and courageous, unafraid of Seven or anyone else."

"My apologies," I said. "I was simply hoping to make you smile."

"Why would you want me to smile?" he asked. "We're on our way to claim the body of the deceased Queen, and you wish me to be lighthearted?"

Well, dang, Reader. Now I felt like a complete jerk.

"Again, I'm sorry."

"You must understand," the Gryphon said, "Alice is a child. This situation would be unnerving for anyone. Surely, Bill, with your exceptional logic and common sense, you realize her attempt at frivolity is a result of her nervousness."

Matthew...my hero.

"Indeed, I do, but she must learn to be properly respectful."

"I am trying, but I imagine you have a lovely smile that could reassure us all that somehow everything will be all right before we get to the Duchess's house." I gave persuading the dragon to show us his teeth my best shot.

"Children must learn that reassurance doesn't usually come with laughter and smiles but with calm restraint." Bill walked on slightly ahead of us.

I shrugged at Vidocq and the Gryphon. The Gryphon gave me a wink of encouragement while Vidocq stuck out his tongue at Bill's back.

Another idea took hold, and I hurried to fall back into

step beside Bill. "You never finished your story of how you became friends with the King."

"Ah, yes, I was assisting the soldiers with the royal rosebushes when the Queen and the King strolled by. The Queen demanded to know what we were doing. Well, the soldiers fell flat on their faces in deference, but I firmly stood my ground."

"Because you refused to be pushed around by anyone ever again," I said.

"That's right. With my head held high, I told the Queen I was helping the soldiers weed the royal garden. It wasn't exactly the truth, but I surmised it was close enough. The Queen continued on her way, but the King remained behind to chat."

Widening my eyes, I said, "I imagine he was impressed by your boldness."

"He was." Bill fell just short of smiling. "After that, the King and I often spoke together near the croquet field or by the garden gate when the Queen wasn't around."

"Did it ever cross your mind to teach the old girl some manners?" Vidocq asked.

"I should say not!" Bill stopped and scowled at Vidocq. "The Queen was nothing to me. I didn't even consider her to be my sovereign. After all, I'm a dragon. I should be living in a kingdom of dragons with one of my peers serving as ruler."

"Do you know where there might be a kingdom of dragons?" I asked.

"Sadly, no."

"Have you looked for one?" Vidocq asked. "If I were in your position, I'd be in no hurry whatsoever to leave Wonderland. Here, you're the sole dragon. Elsewhere, you might not be remarkable in the least."

With a low growl, Bill said, "You're impertinent, and I'd prefer you don't speak to me again until we get to the Duchess's house."

"Sorry." Vidocq's whiskers twitched. "I was making an observation, that's all."

"I believe that the point the Cheshire Cat was trying to make is that you could easily overthrow the government here and make yourself the leader of Wonderland," I said. "The King is lucky you're his friend and that you have no designs on his throne."

"Indeed. I'm an excellent friend." He glared at Vidocq. "And a formidable enemy."

WE ARRIVED at the Duchess's house, and Bill knocked on the door.

Throwing open the door, the Cook asked, "What is it now?"

"We'd like an audience with the Queen," Bill said.

The Duchess appeared at the Cook's side. "Her Majesty has finished her nap and has gone home."

"That's preposterous!" I raced past the Duchess and dodged a pan thrown at me by the Cook.

"Stay out of there!" she yelled. "Get out of this house!"

Ducking out of the way of another pan, I hurried to the bedroom where the Queen had been "resting." She was gone.

I went back to the hallway where the Duchess and the Cook were waiting. "What have you done with her?"

"Nothing whatsoever," the Duchess said. "As I told you, she must have awoken from her nap and returned to the castle."

Turning to the cook, I asked, "'Did *you* do something with the Queen? Did you hide her somewhere?"

Bill stuck his head—the only part of him that would fit—inside the house. "Everyone needs to settle down so we may discuss this matter civilly."

"We have nothing to discuss." The Duchess walked toward Bill making shooing motions with both hands. "The Queen is gone, and it's past time for my supper. Please be on your way, all of you."

"Supper," I said. "My sisters came here to take me home to supper. Do you know where they are now, Duchess?"

"I have no idea. Now, if you'll excuse me, I'd like to have my own meal if Cook will get it finished."

"I'd have had it done long before now had it not been for all the interruptions we've had today." The Cook folded her skinny arms.

"Please forgive our intrusion," Bill said. "We'll be on our way now."

I didn't want to leave, but the Gryphon gave me a

nod. He was right. The Queen wasn't here. There was nothing else we could do.

At least, Bill had been dead-on in saying I shouldn't have brought the King here to see the Queen. Was it a lucky guess, or had he known all along that we wouldn't find the Queen tucked away in the Duchess's guestroom?

Plodding through the Duchess's front door, I thought again of my sisters. "Lorina! I asked her to wait for me."

The Cook slammed the door behind me, and I took off in the direction where I'd last seen Lorina. Bill, the Gryphon, and Vidocq followed me.

I located the fallen log on which Lorina had been sitting, but she wasn't there.

"Lorina!" I called. "Lorina, it's me—Alice! Lorina, are you here?"

There was no response.

Standing in the clearing, I looked all around and continued shouting my sister's name.

"*Ma petite*," Vidocq said, drawing my attention to the log. He held up a piece of torn pale pink fabric.

I rushed over and took the fabric from between his teeth. "Where did you get this?"

"Here. Beside the log."

"This is from the dress Lorina was wearing." My breath caught. "What's happened to her?"

CHAPTER 12

"We have to find Lorina," I said.

"Having no idea who that person is, I shall make sure that the Queen has safely returned to the castle." Bill gave them a slight bow before leaving.

As soon as Bill was out of earshot, the Gryphon said, "Lorina was never even supposed to be *in* Wonderland, and she's trying to get you out as well."

"I agree with the Gryphon." Vidocq edged closer to us. "Finding Lorina isn't conducive to solving the mystery of who killed the Queen, resetting this book, and getting you back to the real world. You must not lose focus, *ma petite*. It's too dangerous."

Expelling a breath, I said, "Lorina is my sister."

"No, Gia, she isn't." The Gryphon rested a talon lightly on my shoulder. "Lorina is—or *was*—Alice Liddell's sister. Whether or not anything bad happens to her in this story, it won't ultimately matter. The best thing you can do for Lorina—and everyone else—is find out who killed the Queen and confront that person so the book will reset."

"I've known from the outset that if a real person dies in Literatia, that person dies in our world too." I looked from the Gryphon to Vidocq. "What if Lorina dies here and it changes something important about the future?"

"Lorina is no longer living in the real world and, thus, exists only in Literatia," the Gryphon said.

"Like me." Vidocq spoke quietly. "I can no longer be in your world." Then he lifted his chin. "But I can move around very well in Literatia."

The Gryphon tightened his grip on my shoulder. "You're the one in real danger because of your unstable size. We don't know what might happen to you next."

"I haven't changed sizes for several minutes."

"That doesn't mean you're stable," Vidocq said.

"All right." I sighed again. "But I still feel compelled to find Lorina. What if Edith or another silverfish did something to her? Or what if she has been taken by the Queen's killer?"

The Gryphon released my shoulder and turned to Vidocq. "That *is* a valid point."

"*Oui.*"

Buoyed by their concession, I said, "We'll find Lorina and make sure she's okay and that she hasn't fallen prey to Edith or some other villain, and then we'll resume our search for the Queen. Who knows? The person Lorina is with might've taken the Queen's body, especially if she's with the Queen's killer."

Vidocq shook his head. "I think not. Why would the killer want to take the body now after originally leaving it out in a meadow to be found by anyone who happened upon it?"

"I don't know." I rubbed my forehead. "The Duchess didn't act too suspiciously, but the Cook did. She was throwing pans at me as I ran to the bedroom. It's possible she had something to do with the Queen's disappearance."

"I will stay here and keep watch." Vidocq disappeared, with the exception of his face. "If the Duchess or the Cook have hidden the Queen's body, they will likely speak of it when they believe themselves to be alone. Plus, I can search the house thoroughly."

"That's an excellent idea," the Gryphon said.

"*Merci*. After I have exhausted my efforts here, I will come in search of the two of you. If you find Lorina and all is well with her, return here. Together, we will determine what our next steps should be."

"That's reasonable." I smiled slightly. "Thank you both. I know you think I'm being foolish, but I appreciate your humoring me."

Vidocq disappeared the rest of the way, and we heard him scrambling into the Duchess's house through the window.

"I hope Lorina is all right." I looked down at the fabric

clutched in my hand. "She seemed to truly care about Alice."

"Whatever happened to her—if anything—isn't your fault."

"Yes, it is. I asked Lorina to wait here for me."

Nodding his head forward, the Gryphon said, "Come on." As I fell into step beside him, he continued. "You aren't responsible for the damage the silverfish have done to *Alice's Adventures in Wonderland*. Lorina was never meant to be here."

"But still, she was waiting here for *me*...to take me home," I said. "I never had a sister—or a brother either, for that matter—but I imagine it would have been really nice. After my mom died, I think I'd have enjoyed having someone else who was my family, someone who'd be there for me and who I could support and care for."

"You have that now. Granted, it's an unconventional family, but we love you—me, Vidocq, Cooper, Josephine. Me, in particular. In fact, I'd kiss you if you weren't a little girl and I didn't have a beak."

I laughed. "Sorry. I didn't mean to get maudlin. I'm scared for Lorina, that's all. Even though some of the characters of this world are cardboard playing cards, they're still very real here in Wonderland."

"Oh, I know they are," he said. "Never underestimate a fictional character. There is no limit to what that character might do."

"I know." I walked quietly by his side for a moment. "You know what Vidocq said about being unable to exist in our world—is he sure? What would happen if he was able to go into our world?"

He didn't answer me.

"Matthew?"

Taking a deep breath, he said, "Vidocq would turn to dust. The man died in 1857 in our world. The Vidocq you interact with here in Literatia is, for all intents and purposes, a spirit."

"You mean, he's a ghost?"

"No. Here's he's like us—more so than I'd realized at first." He glanced over at me. "I didn't know Vidocq could transform into a character the way we do. In our previous encounters, he has been simply…Vidocq."

"True. But Wonderland is different from anywhere else," I said.

"I agree." He chuckled softly.

Now that I was certain he was Matthew, I asked, "How is Cooper?"

"Amazing. We had a terrific month, thanks to you."

"A month?" I stopped and stared up at him. "I've been here a *month*?"

"Not exactly. It was a month from the time you left *A Tale of Two Cities* until you turned up here."

"How is that possible? I thought I went immediately from one book to the other."

"No, it only felt that way to you. You were in a state of animated suspension—let's just say you were sleeping— that makes it easier to digest."

"Not much," I mumbled. "But enough about that, tell me about your time with Cooper."

"You gave us a beautiful gift, Gia, and I can't thank you enough."

We began walking again.

"I was, and still am, sad that I missed so much of my son's life," he said. "We shared many key moments through photos and videos while we were together, and we made new memories as well. We even took some selfies, and Josephine took a great photo of us together in the library."

"I'd love to see it," I said.

"You will." He shook his head. "I'd given up hope of ever seeing my son this side of Heaven. Thank you for making that happen for us."

"I'm delighted I was able to reunite the two of you. We have to make sure you spend more time together. Your being apart should be the exception, not the norm." I blinked back tears. "Lorina reminded me of my mom— not in appearance but in the gentle way she spoke to me, her caring manner. Time lost can never be recaptured."

"I know that all too well, sweetheart."

Patting his shoulder, I said, "I'm sorry for all the time you and Cooper lost."

"We both know that it's best to never dwell in the past but to embrace the present and look forward to the future."

I gave him a brief side hug before we walked on. "I

hope we're able to find Lorina before it gets dark. It feels as if this day has gone on forever."

"It has," he said. "It *will*. Have you forgotten that time has stopped in Wonderland?"

"I *had* forgotten that. It's perpetually teatime, right?"

He nodded. "Around six o'clock in the evening."

"Thank goodness we aren't on Daylight Savings Time here." My laughter caught in my throat as I heard something rustling in the bushes. "Did you hear that?"

In lieu of answering, the Gryphon moved to stand in front of me. "Lorina, is that you?"

There was no response.

"Lorina!" I called. "It's me, Alice!"

"Not Lorina," a shaky voice said.

"Don't be afraid! It's all right!" I moved to stand beside rather than behind the Gryphon.

Edith emerged from the bushes, her face scratched and bleeding. In that instant, I forgot she was a silverfish and saw only a hurt child.

"Oh, Edith!"

She came running and threw herself into my arms. I could barely hear the Gryphon's low voice over Edith's sobbing.

"Careful."

"Right." I held her at arm's length. "Edith, what happened?"

"Something terrible has happened to Lorina. You must come with me to help her."

"What is it?" I asked. "What's the terrible thing?"

"The soldiers came and got her," Edith said. "The King is threatening to cut off her head."

"For what reason?" the Gryphon asked.

"I don't know. That's why I need Alice's help."

"We'll all go together." The Gryphon drew himself up to look more imposing than ever.

"I'm not sure that is a good idea." Edith squinted up at him. "You might frighten the soldiers and make them harm Lorina."

"When we get there, I'll assure them I mean them no harm. Besides, shouldn't they be accustomed to me? I've done the Queen's bidding for ages."

"Oh," she said. "I suppose you're right."

"Lead the way," he said.

As Edith walked ahead of us, the Gryphon and I shared a glance. I didn't know what we were doing, but I trusted the Gryphon had a plan.

At least, I hoped he did because, Reader, I was at a complete loss.

CHAPTER 13

The Gryphon stopped, drawing me closer to his side with a talon. "We'll never catch up to the soldiers at this rate. They're too far ahead of us. Let's turn back the way we came and meet them at the castle."

"We can't." Edith looked from the Gryphon to me and back again. "I mean, what if they hurt Lorina?"

"Why would they hurt her?" I asked. "You said the King is threatening to cut off her head. Everyone knows the King is always the one who negates the Queen's orders of head-chopping. He won't hurt Lorina."

"The King is different now," she said.

"Why is that?" It was hard to keep my face impassive when I felt as if we'd backed Edith into a corner. Was she about to reveal her true self to us?

"Because the Queen is dead. He holds all the power now." She raised her chin.

"That's ridiculous." I scoffed. "No one believes the

Queen is dead. In fact, the Duchess just told the Gryphon and me that the Queen had finished resting and returned to the castle."

"That's a lie. You and I saw the Queen as plain as day, and we know she's dead." Edith regarded me with a shrewdness that belied her supposed age. "Her head was ripped off, for goodness' sake."

I looked at the Gryphon, but his face was unreadable.

Reader, I imagine the expressions of mythical creatures would be hard to read under the most ideal circumstances, and this situation was far from ideal.

"What do you suggest we do?" I asked Edith. "Our... um...friend, Bill the Dragon, just set off looking for the Queen, who was at the Duchess's home the last time we saw her." I rubbed my forehead. "For a dead person, she sure does get around."

Before Edith could answer, the Gryphon said, "Let's go to the castle and confront the soldiers there."

"No!" Edith cried. "Do you *want* the soldiers to throw Alice in the dungeon with Lorina?"

"Of course not. Why would they do that?" The Gryphon's piercing eyes bore into hers. "You said you didn't know why the soldiers took Lorina. Is that true?"

Sighing, she said, "It's not. They accused Lorina of conspiring with Alice to murder the Queen."

"Then we shall convince the King that Lorina and Alice are innocent," the Gryphon said.

"He'll never listen to reason," she said. "He believes whatever he chooses, and that's that."

"The Cheshire Cat is persuasive," I said. "It's possible he could argue our case before the King."

Edith glared at me. "To what end?"

"To make him understand that neither Lorina nor I had anything to do with the Queen's murder and that we volunteer to help him discover who did." I smiled. "Shall we go find the Cat?"

"Absolutely." The Gryphon gave a definitive nod. "Let's go."

Stamping her foot, Edith said, "We don't need to find a cat. We need to find Lorina. She needs us."

"It would be unwise for two little girls and a Gryphon to take on an entire battalion of soldiers." The Gryphon started to turn, making sure to place himself between me and Edith. "We'll locate the Cheshire Cat and then go on to the castle to request an audience with the King."

"I don't like your plan!"

Ignoring Edith, the Gryphon kept the two of us moving back in the direction of the Duchess's home.

"I said, I don't like your plan!"

"Then do as you wish," the Gryphon said over his shoulder.

I was holding my breath, Reader. What would she do? Go the other way? Follow us? Stab us in the back? She was currently in the form of a helpless little girl, but she was in truth a silverfish and could take on another form.

I glanced at the Gryphon from the corner of my eye. He was stoically marching forward, shielding me from

Edith. Straining my ears, I heard her clomping along behind us.

How I wished I could speak privately with the Gryphon—to ask him what he was thinking. Did he have a plan? How could he? Neither of us had expected to encounter Edith. We were both playing this entire composition by ear.

UPON ARRIVING outside the Duchess's house, the Gryphon stopped. "Cheshire Cat, are you here?"

I understood that the Gryphon wasn't calling *Vidocq* because Edith was here. Hopefully, Vidocq would take the hint.

"Up here."

We looked up to see Vidocq crouched in a tree.

"We were wondering if perhaps you saw the Queen from your lofty perch," the Gryphon said.

Vidocq stood, stretched, and climbed down from the tree. "I have not. However, when the two of you passed by earlier, you were talking about a girl who'd gone missing. I see that you found her."

He knew this girl was Edith and not Lorina, and I was glad he was playing his part so well.

"Actually, this is my sister, Edith," I said. "She told us that the King's soldiers have taken our older sister, Lorina."

"I see. Is the King seeking an opponent to play croquet?"

"No, you stupid cat." Edith rolled her eyes. "Lorina has been accused of killing the Queen."

"But the Queen isn't dead," Vidocq said. "Everyone except Alice knows that, you rude little girl."

"*I* know it," Edith said. "And Alice needs to come with me immediately to save Lorina."

Vidocq narrowed his eyes to slits. "Why are you convinced the Queen is dead? Did you kill her?"

The Gryphon and I watched their exchange as if we were observing a tennis match.

"Don't be absurd," she said. "Why would I harm the Queen?"

"You tell me—why *did* you harm the Queen?"

"I didn't!" Edith uttered a shriek of frustration.

"Then why do you insist some harm has befallen her?" Vidocq walked around Edith in a slow circle.

"Because someone ripped her head from her body. I saw it lying next to her on the bed." Edith sounded nothing like the child she was pretending to be. "And if Alice and I don't rescue Lorina, she's likely to suffer the same fate."

"You're awfully bold to believe you can save your sister from an army," Vidocq said.

"I made that point myself," the Gryphon said. "And recalling how persuasive you can be, I thought you might go to the castle with us to encourage the King to let Lorina go."

"I could do that." Vidocq turned his attention back to Edith. "Provided your sister did not, in fact, injure the Queen. Are you sure she did not?"

"Y-yes."

"How do you know? Have you been with her all day?" he asked.

Edith shrugged. "Not all day but for most of it."

"Ah." Vidocq inclined his head. "You are, then, an unreliable witness. Either you and/or one—perhaps even *both* of your sisters—might have set upon the Queen like a gang of brigands, and you expect *me* to risk my credibility by vouching for you before the King?"

I began to worry that Vidocq was playing his part too well and that he wasn't planning on going to the castle with us. Had he learned something that had convinced him to stay here and continue staking out the Duchess's house? Or was he simply trying to badger a confession out of Edith?

"Um…Mr. Cheshire Cat," I began, "are you declining our request to accompany us to the castle?"

"I've not yet made up my mind," he said. "I have more questions for this obnoxious child first. Why did the soldiers leave you behind when they took your sister?"

"I hid," Edith said, "Never mind about these two, Alice. They aren't going to help us. Let's go home and get Papa. He'll go with us to save Lorina."

"No." I shook my head. "Papa would be angry that we allowed Lorina to get into trouble. We have to save her before we go home."

Edith tried to take my hand, but I moved away.

Squinting at me, she asked, "Why won't you take my hand, sister? I'm frightened."

"Are you being honest with me?" I put my hands on my hips so she wouldn't reach for me again. "Did the soldiers *really* take Lorina away?"

"Yes!" She lowered her eyes. "But Lorina is older, bigger, and stronger than either of us. She might have been able to free herself. That's why we need to follow the path taken by the soldiers."

"Very well," Vidocq said. "You and I will take the route of the soldiers. Alice and the Gryphon can go ahead to the castle. The four of us—or five, should we find Lorina —will meet there."

"No. I want to be with Alice," Edith said. "She and I will follow the soldiers, and the two of you may meet *us* at the castle."

As I was attempting to come up with a viable protest, I shrank. Not just a little, but enough for Edith to grab me and take off running through the forest.

CHAPTER 14

Edith was surprisingly fast. Or maybe she only seemed to be racing like she had gasoline running through her veins because I was tiny and clenched in her fist. Either way, I wished she'd simply stop.

"Where are you taking me?" I struggled to pry open her hand but realized that if I managed to get free and she dropped me, the fall could very well kill me. I stilled.

"Home where you belong." She looked back over her shoulder.

I wondered how close the Gryphon and Vidocq were, but I didn't dare ask. Surely as a silverfish, Edith knew she could easily destroy me in my fragile state. Either the thought hadn't yet occurred to her, or the Gryphon and Vidocq were too close for her to risk stopping and killing me.

What should I do? I might be able to get that last bite of mushroom out of my pocket and into my mouth, but would it make me grow or shrink even more? The Caterpillar had indicated that eating the rest of the mushroom would stabilize my size fluctuations; but if I stayed my current size, what use would it be to me? However, if I didn't give it a try, I felt as if I were giving up and putting my fate squarely in Edith's hands.

Feeling I had little to lose, I dug the morsel from my pocket, whispered a prayer, and ate the mushroom.

Reader, I grew.

My growth spurt caused Edith's hand—made up of a conglomeration of silverfish—to explode. As I landed on my feet in the grass, silverfish ran every which way. I brushed them off my arms and legs and shook out my hair in case any silverfish had managed to land on my head.

Turning to look at Edith, I saw that there wasn't an Edith anymore. When her hand had blown apart, so had the rest of her. Where she'd been, there were now thousands of silverfish scattering in all directions.

I whirled to see where the Gryphon and Vidocq were. They weren't behind me. Just as I was about to panic, the Gryphon swooped down and picked me up with one talon. He was clutching Vidocq in the other.

The Gryphon flew back to a part of the forest near the home of the March Hare. As he put Vidocq and me on the ground, he asked, "Are you all right?"

"Perhaps a teensy bit bruised from your strong grip," Vidocq said, "but, *oui*, I am fine. Besides, I prefer a bruise to having to fight a legion of silverfish."

"I'm okay too." I checked my arms and legs again. "You don't see any of those nasty things on me, do you?"

Both my companions assured me that I was silverfish free, as far as they could see.

"How did you grow?" the Gryphon asked. "Was it pure luck?"

"Not exactly. I ate the remainder of the mushroom. If what the Caterpillar told us is true, then I should stay the size I am now." I frowned. "Right?"

"Let's hope so." The Gryphon gave me a reassuring pat on the shoulder.

"Do we believe what Edith said about the soldiers taking Lorina?" Vidocq asked. "Is it possible the King's men really took her?"

"Anything is possible." I put both hands on my head and vigorously rubbed my scalp. "Sorry, but I had never seen that many silverfish in one place in my life, and it's freaking me out."

"Understandable." The Gryphon surveyed the area around us. "We need to keep moving. Soon those silver-fish are going to reassemble—into Edith or into something else entirely. When that happens, I'd like for us to be well on our way to the castle."

"Agreed," I said. "And whether or not the soldiers took Lorina, we were planning on going to see the King anyway."

"Vidocq, did you hear anything useful at the Duchess's house?" the Gryphon asked.

"I learned only that the Queen was definitely not in

the house. The women didn't speak of her again. In fact, they spoke of nothing except supper."

"So, even if the Cook was responsible for moving the Queen's body, it appears the Duchess, at least, had nothing to do with it," I said.

"*Exactement.* I would wager that the Cook and the King's soldiers took the Queen," Vidocq said.

"Do you think they intend to keep up the ruse that the Queen isn't dead?" I fell into step beside the Gryphon who was urging us onward.

"I do not know, but I imagine we'll find out once we arrive at the castle." Vidocq leapt into my arms. "I wouldn't want my languid steps to slow our procession."

I laughed. "Lazy cat."

WE STOPPED a short distance from the castle to get our plan fleshed out before approaching the King.

Placing Vidocq gently onto the ground, I said, "I feel I should be our spokesperson. The King will expect me to speak because it was I who led him into the clearing to discover that the Queen's body was no longer there."

"I recall your saying he was angry and thought you'd tricked him," Vidocq said. "But I was there. I, too, saw the Queen lying in the meadow and later at the Duchess's house."

"What about Bill?" the Gryphon asked. "Do we believe him to be a friend or a foe?"

"It's hard to say." I mulled over the issue. "I don't get the impression he's a silverfish, but he *is* full of self-importance. I get the feeling his leap from Bill the Lizard to Bill the Dragon has made him power-hungry, and I imagine he'll go along with whatever the King wants."

"Perhaps we can make Bill realize he is even more eminent than the King," Vidocq said. "After all, the King is merely a playing card, *non*? Bill is a magnificent dragon."

"Good luck with that," the Gryphon said. "In my opinion, our best bet is to request to see the Queen. After all, Alice, you owe Her Majesty an apology for inadvertently spreading the falsehood that she was dead."

"Oh, that's good." I smiled. "Yes, that's an excellent idea. Let's go."

The Gryphon's plan was inspired. By asking to visit with the Queen, who we'd been told had returned to the castle, we could undo the damage I'd already done by announcing to the King that his wife was dead. He'd have to make up an excuse as to why the Queen couldn't see us, or else he'd have to admit that she was dead.

As we neared the castle gate, two guards—Nine and Four—blocked our way.

"We've been told to keep you out, prankster," Nine said. "Move along."

"Oh, please allow me to come in and apologize to the Queen and King," I said. "I never intended to deceive the King or to spread the inaccurate account of the Queen's death. I was mistaken—very likely *deceived*—myself."

"We have our orders," Four said.

"Won't you be a dear and ask the King if he'll reconsider?" I did my best to look guileless, stopping just short of batting my eyes. "Or if you won't, could you tell me if my friend, Bill the Dragon, is still here?"

Nine raised his brows. "You're an acquaintance of Bill's?"

I nodded.

"We'll see about that," he said. "Bill!"

Momentarily, Bill ambled to the gate. "Hello. You called for me?"

"Yes. This little girl claims to be your friend," Nine said.

"I suppose she is. We took a stroll to search for the Queen a short time ago. Her Majesty had been at the Duchess's house but had left by the time we arrived." Bill looked at me. "Did you find your sister?"

"I'm afraid not," I said. "I was told she might be here, but these gentlemen won't allow us to come inside. I owe both the Queen and the King an apology. Could *you* escort us into the royal garden? The soldiers must know that no one would be capable of making any trouble with a dragon around."

"We have orders from the King to keep you out," Four reminded me yet again.

"But only—I imagine—because he thought I would return to make mischief," I said. "I have no intention of doing so. I humbly ask you to at least ask the King if he will see me."

"Come now, Four." Bill loomed over the two soldiers. "I will take responsibility for the girl and her friends and will see to it that neither of you get into trouble for disobeying orders. Open the gate."

The soldiers looked at each other. Nine shrugged and opened the gate.

"Thank you ever so much," I said.

Both of them ignored me.

Bill preceded us into the garden where the King sat at tea.

"What is *she* doing here?" The King stood, nearly upsetting his teacup as he did so.

"I'm here to apologize, Your Majesty." I curtsied. "Please forgive me for my hysterical antics earlier today. I mistakenly believed the Queen had been harmed. I had honorable reasons for coming to you."

"What the girl says is true," Vidocq said. "She and I saw the Queen in the meadow and thought she was hurt. We didn't realize she was merely resting."

"Very well." The King sat back down. "I accept your apology."

"Thank you." I smiled. "May I please apologize to the Queen now?"

Arching a brow, the King said, "The Queen is in her chambers preparing for a croquet match at the moment."

"May I please stay and watch the game?" I asked.

"That isn't necessary." The King's smile was more of a grimace. "I will be happy to pass along your apology to the Queen."

"Oh, but I *love* croquet." I looked around the garden. "Is it true that you play with flamingos for mallets and hedgehogs for balls?"

Reader, I didn't see any flamingos or hedgehogs, and I was glad. I thought it was mean to use the animals that way.

"Of course, we do," the King said. "How else would one play croquet?"

"Please give me permission to remain here and watch the game," I said. "I understand if you'd prefer I don't speak with the Queen after the trouble I've caused today, but I would enjoy watching the match."

"Fine." He looked around for one of his soldiers. "Three, go up and see if the Queen is ready for the croquet match."

"Alice's younger sister, Edith, told us earlier that their older sister, Lorina, was here at the castle," Vidocq said. "Is she perhaps the Queen's opponent in the match?"

"I don't know anyone named Lorina." The King frowned at me. "Nor have I seen any other girls like *you* here pestering me and my staff today."

Three returned, looked at the Gryphon, Vidocq, and me, and then bent to whisper in the King's ear.

A sliver of dread snaked down my spine.

"What?" the King asked. "Are you quite sure?"

"Positive, Your Majesty," Three said.

Pointing at me, the King shouted, "Seize her! She killed the Queen!"

CHAPTER 15

Before the guards could take me into custody, the Gryphon grabbed me and flew over the garden wall. Amid the shouted directives of their King, the soldiers scrambled into action.

The Gryphon was rising higher into the sky, and I closed my eyes against the gust of wind. I heard him grunt in pain, and I mustered up the nerve to look down. There were archers below us.

"Are you hit?" I cried.

"I'm fine." His voice was terse and strained. He was definitely not fine.

"Land somewhere. Don't let them shoot you again."

He ignored me.

I felt the draft off an arrow that barely missed us. "Matthew...*please.*"

A sharp intake of breath told me that another arrow had found its mark. He snarled, set me down on the top of a building half hidden by a strand of trees, and then led the soldiers away from me.

Putting both hands over my mouth to silence my scream, I watched in horror as the Gryphon's arrow-riddled body began its descent. The soldiers raced to find the site where he'd landed.

I hid on the roof and wept, feeling like a coward. I didn't know what to do or how to help Matthew, and I'd never felt so despondent in my life. He'd risked his life to save me. If I ran out into the open now, everything he'd done would be in vain.

But what if Matthew died? No! I refused to believe that. I *couldn't* believe it. He had to be all right.

Reader, it was obvious he wasn't all right, but I had to find him. I had to save him somehow. I just had to escape the soldiers to do it.

I'd look for the Caterpillar. Maybe he could give me another magic mushroom, and I could eat enough to make myself a giant. That way, I could crush all those stupid playing cards, gather up Matthew, and take him home. I didn't even care about this book anymore. Let the silverfish have it. It wasn't more important than Matthew.

Climbing down one of the trees, I realized I'd been atop the White Rabbit's house. Would there be any clue inside the house as to where I might find the Caterpillar? Before I could check and see, I heard a voice behind me.

"There you are."

It was Lorina, and she breathed a sigh of relief. "I saw

the Gryphon get shot down, and I was beside myself with worry."

"So am I. We need to find him immediately."

"Find who, dear?" she asked.

Looking at her as if she'd lost her mind, I said, "The Gryphon. He was shot down protecting me."

"Forget about that. Simply wake up, Alice, and end this nightmare."

"I wish it was that easy, but it isn't. I can't save Matthew—I mean, the Gryphon—if I wake up."

"Perhaps not, but you can leave Wonderland behind you forever."

"I won't do that," I said. "I won't turn my back on him."

Lorina dropped to her knees in front of me and took both my hands. "I can't protect you while you're here in Wonderland. I need to get you back home where I can keep you safe for as long as possible."

"I truly appreciate that you appear to have my best interests at heart, but I absolutely won't leave Wonderland until I find the Gryphon and make sure he's safe." I took a steadying breath. "Will you help me?"

"Of course." Lorina stood and took my hand.

"You haven't seen the Caterpillar around, have you?" I asked.

"The who?"

I shook my head. "Never mind."

We walked slowly, keeping an eye out for feathers or blood or anything that would lead us to where the

Gryphon had landed. I also scanned the area for splashes of blue or a plume of smoke, but I didn't see any sign of the Caterpillar either.

"Oh, my."

At Lorina's soft exclamation, I whipped my head in the direction she was looking. There was a large patch of high grass that had been flattened, but the Gryphon was not there. Some of his feathers were there, and there was blood, but no Gryphon.

"Where is he?" My voice broke as I choked on the sob that rose in my throat. "He has to be here. He must have gotten up and walked away."

"I don't think so," she said. "There's no trail leading away from this spot. It appears the soldiers found him before we did and took him back to the castle."

"That's impossible," I said. "We'd have met them had that been the case."

"Not if they took a different route back to the castle."

I made a slow turn to decide which way to go. Making up my mind, I headed into the forest. That's where Matthew would go to hide. There wasn't a trail because he'd flown there. Yes, that had to be it.

"Alice, come back!"

I ignored her. She meant well—probably—but Matthew was hurt, and he needed me. I picked up my pace until I was running.

"Run faster!"

It was Lorina's changing her tune that made me

stumble. I stopped, looked back at her and saw the soldiers racing to surround me.

Faltering had been my downfall. I found myself standing amid a circle of soldiers who were pointing spears at me.

"The Gryphon—what have you done with him?" I asked. "Is he going to be all right?"

"We haven't seen him," one said. "We don't care about the Gryphon. It's *you* we were ordered to capture."

"Please find him, make sure he's all right, and then let him go," I said. "If you'll do that, I'll peaceably surrender to you."

He pressed the tip of his spear to my throat. "You will do that anyway, if you know what's good for you."

"I'll search for him, Alice," Lorina said. "You have my word."

"Thank you." I wasn't terribly reassured, but I supposed her offer to look for the Gryphon was better than nothing. And it was all I had at the moment.

BACK AT THE CASTLE, the soldiers bypassed the garden completely and shuffled me into a musty, shadowy dungeon. They jostled me down a narrow hallway and shoved me into a tiny cell. The heavy door clanged shut behind me.

I peered out of the small, barred window for a moment, but when I saw no indication that neither the

King nor anyone else was going to speak with me, I sat on the cold concrete floor.

There was nothing in this cell—no cot, no sink, nothing. And whereas the rest of Wonderland was an exaggeration of colors and fantastical elements, here there was nothing but gray. Harsh. Empty. Dreadful. Colorless.

Did the soldiers—or, rather, the King—plan on leaving me here? Was I going to die in this place?

No, Reader, I absolutely was not! I was going to come up with a brilliant plan to escape, save Matthew, and maybe even discover who killed the Queen in order to reset this book.

I got up and tried the door. Of course, that was a useless endeavor, but I figured it didn't hurt to try at least once. I imagined playing card soldiers weren't too bright. It wasn't beyond the realm of possibility that they'd forgotten to lock the door. No such luck.

As I roamed around my dingy box, I thought about the symbolism contained in *Alice's Adventures in Wonderland*. The Queen represented rules and rigidity, not to mention tyranny. She was the character Alice was forced to confront before she was able to wake up from her dream.

Lorina had known Alice needed to wake up. But had Alice not awakened on her own in the story, would she have dealt with her issues of growing up, resolved them, and been ready to move into adulthood? I couldn't imagine that Lewis Carroll would have let the story end with the Queen executing Alice, rather than have the child wake up beside her sister on the riverbank.

Still, the silverfish had damaged the original manuscript, making Wonderland a much more sinister place. Now anything could happen. Alice—*I*—really could be executed.

Remembering the book I'd taken from the White Rabbit's house, I retrieved it from my pocket.

Secrets in Wonderland.

Hopefully, one of the *secrets* would be how to escape this dungeon.

Chapter One: Maps and Passages – How to Get Anywhere in Wonderland with the Least Amount of Effort

Skimming the chapter, I saw nothing that would aid me in getting out of this cell. But if I did manage to get out, I could possibly use one or more of the secret passageways located in the book to escape the garden and find the Gryphon.

Chapter Two: The Magical and Medicinal – Plants Native to Wonderland

Having nothing else to do but wait, I read this chapter and learned that pink four-leaf clovers had incredible healing properties and could typically be found along the outer walls of the palace garden. Good to know.

Chapter Three: Creatures Great and Small – Known Inhabitants of Wonderland

I wondered if the addition of silverfish had altered this book in any way. Since *Secrets in Wonderland* was a book within a book, I wasn't sure how that might work.

Hearing footsteps, I shoved the book back into my pocket and hurried to the door and peered out the tiny window. The two of clubs was heading in my direction and was carrying a teacup on a saucer.

"If you would please step to the far corner of the cell, I will bring in your tea," he said.

I hurried to the back wall. Could I rush him after he unlocked the door? If I did, what would I do next? I needed a weapon and to know where the guards were.

Two unlocked the door, eased inside the cell, and—without taking his eyes off me—placed the cup gently onto the floor.

"What is that?" I asked.

"Tea. It's teatime, you know."

"Yes, but is it poison?"

"I don't believe so," he said.

"When is my trial? All of this is so very confusing to me."

He was backing toward the door. "I don't know."

"First, I found the Queen lying in a meadow and thought she was dead." I kept my back to the wall, not wanting to frighten Two anymore than he was already. "Everyone else told me the Queen was fine, and I should have listened to them. Instead, I came here to tell the King. We went to look for her, couldn't find her, and he called me a cruel prankster."

"Oh, dear," Two said.

"So, when it appeared that the Queen had been alive all along—" As if I believed that for a second. "—then I returned here to apologize to both the Queen and the King for the trouble I'd caused. Then the King accuses me of *killing* the Queen and throws me into the dungeon. Does that make any sense to you?"

"No." He shrugged. "Very little makes sense to me. I'm of the lowest rank, and no one expects me to question anything. Therefore, I never do."

"You might not have questions, sir, but I certainly do. Will you please ask the King if he will come and see me? Or, if not, will he have me brought before him to plead my case?"

"Yes, I will pass along your message," Two said. "I wouldn't get my hopes up if I were you. The King isn't likely to listen to me." He backed the rest of the way out of the cell and locked the door back.

CHAPTER 16

There was no way I was going to drink that tea without knowing exactly what it was or what it would do to me. Had there been a grate in the floor, I would have poured it out, but there wasn't even that in this barren cell.

Hearing Two's footsteps fade, I wondered if he'd even try to give the King my message. I hoped he would at least return for the teacup, and I could knock him down and take my chances with whatever guards may be outside.

I went back to the window but could see nothing but the empty hallway. But *was* the hallway empty? Playing cards were thin, they could flatten themselves against any wall.

Turning back toward the inside of the cell, I saw Vidocq materializing. Gasping, I said his name.

"Shhh! You must speak quietly," he whispered. "I

followed Two into the cell, and I'll disappear if we hear anyone coming."

"Did you find Matthew?"

"*Non.* I opted to stay with you. Bill went searching for the Gryphon. He knows you are innocent and even tried to speak with the King on your behalf, but the King wouldn't listen. When the King sent the soldiers after you and the Gryphon, Bill and I followed. We saw the Gryphon shot down."

"Then why couldn't you find him?" I asked. "Lorina and I found where he'd landed, but he was gone. I hoped he was able to fly into the forest and hide, but the soldiers caught me before I could search for him. Lorina said she'd continue looking for him, but I'm not sure I trust her."

"Trust *no one* in Wonderland, *ma petite.*"

"You say that, and yet, you trust Bill?"

"*Touche.* I do trust Bill to a certain extent. I hope he found Matthew and that Lorina did not," he said.

"I get the feeling Lorina truly cares about Alice."

"As Alice's sister, there is a strong possibility that she does indeed care for Alice. She does not care for the Gryphon, *n'est-ce pas?*"

Sighing, I said, "That's true. Do you think the King will grant me an audience? If I can get him to confess to me that he murdered the Queen, then maybe we can all get out of this book."

"One, I find it highly unlikely that the King will grant

you an audience; and two, what makes you sure it was he who killed the Queen?"

"Well, I don't think the Duchess did. Do you?"

"I don't think so, but I have no evidence that she did or did not," he said.

Rubbing my temples with my index and middle fingers, I decided Vidocq was starting to make about as much sense as the real Cheshire Cat. "Look, how many guards are out there?"

"There are two guarding each of the exits, but I didn't see any in the hallways. That said, if you can get out of the cell, I don't know how you'll get out of the dungeon."

"All right. Is there any way you can squeeze through those bars?"

Vidocq's eyes widened. "I am not an overly fat cat, but I cannot fit through there."

"Okay, but if you *are* able to get out before I can get out, would you do me a favor?"

"Anything for you." He gave me a courtly bow.

"Please see if you can find both Matthew and the Caterpillar," I said.

"The Caterpillar?"

"Yes. If I can become gigantic, I can safely get us all out of here."

He took a deep breath. "I believe it to be unwise to play around with those freaky mushrooms, *ma petite*."

"I know, Vidocq, but I'm about out of options."

Upon our hearing footsteps in the hallway, Vidocq faded until he was completely invisible.

Two came to the door. "The King said to let you know he will hear your defense at your trial tomorrow morning."

"Thank you." I walked to the back of the cell. "Would you please come and retrieve this teacup?"

"Yes." Two unlocked the door, grabbed the teacup, and made a hasty exit.

"You could be a dear and leave the door unlocked."

"I'm sorry. I—"

"Please find me a magic mushroom!" I was making my request to Vidocq, who I was sure had slipped out the door.

"I do wish I could help you, miss," Two said. "However, I cannot without…you know."

"I know."

The sound of the tumblers turning in the lock assured me that Two had not left the door unlocked. I prayed Vidocq would find a way to help Matthew—and me, but primarily, Matthew.

Tomorrow morning was to be my trial. Yet, the clocks had stopped in Wonderland. There would be no tomorrow.

I DON'T KNOW how long I sat on the numbing concrete floor before I heard a key rattling in the lock once more. I stood. If Two had returned with another cup of tea, I was going to push past him and escape this time.

The door swung open. To my surprise, my visitor wasn't Two, it was the White Rabbit. It occurred to me that this was the first time I'd seen him.

"Come with me," he said quietly. "We haven't much time."

I followed the White Rabbit out of the cell. I didn't necessarily trust the rabbit, but he was letting me out of the cell. For that, I was grateful.

He closed the door and locked it back.

"Where are you taking me?" I asked. "To the King?"

"No. To the Gryphon."

"Is he all right?"

"He has a broken wing, but he'll be fine."

"How did—"

The White Rabbit glared at me. "No more talking."

I didn't say anything else, but the questions still swirled around in my mind. Was the White Rabbit truly trustworthy? I could distinctly hear Vidocq's voice saying in my head, *trust no one in Wonderland*. And yet, we'd both trusted characters here. But why would the White Rabbit show up out of nowhere to help me?

He led me down the dungeon's dimly lit corridors, constantly on the lookout for guards. We passed other cells—some empty and others containing other Wonderland characters. The Knave of Hearts—if I'd been unfamiliar with the story, I'd have thought he was the Jack—was in one cell.

"Get me out of here!" he shouted, as we passed his cell.

"Be quiet and we'll come back for you," the White Rabbit said.

The Dodo was in another cell, but he seemed perfectly content. Was that because he'd created this world and was happy no matter what was happening within it? Or was there some other reason he was at ease in a prison cell of his own making?

I didn't have much of a chance to ponder the matter because the White Rabbit stopped in front of a door.

"Quietly follow me, closing the door behind you." He pulled a large keyring from his pocket and unlocked the door.

The dungeon had been brightly illuminated compared to this narrow hallway in which I now stood with the White Rabbit.

"This way." He took out a flashlight. "It's a maze. You must stay close to me at all times."

"All right." I took a step to the right of the White Rabbit.

He jerked my arm, causing me to trip and fall to the ground in front of him as a wall of spikes thrust down from the ceiling.

I gasped. "Those would have impaled me!"

"Yes." He sighed. "Stay directly behind me. We have got to get you out of this book before you get us all killed."

"Who are you really?" I asked.

"Shush. We have to hurry. Escape now, talk later."

I wondered if Vidocq had somehow managed to

shapeshift into the rabbit, but the White Rabbit didn't really talk like Vidocq. If Matthew had transformed into the White Rabbit, he wouldn't be taking me to the Gryphon, and he'd have assured me that he was fine. Nor would either of the men been so brusque with me.

Was this a trick? Was the White Rabbit like the Butterfly, who was trying to trick me into abandoning Literatia?

"Get down like this." The White Rabbit dropped onto all fours and crawled through a tunnel.

What choice did I have? I followed him. I'd decide what to do when I learned what situation I found myself in next.

The White Rabbit opened a trapdoor. I squinted at the sudden brightness as I followed him to the surface.

As my eyes adjusted to the sunlight, I realized the White Rabbit and I were in a part of the garden thick with rose trees. I remembered that in the original manuscript, the rose trees were at the entrance of the garden.

"We've made it," I whispered.

"Not yet." He pulled me with him as he ducked to avoid being seen by a guard patrolling the grounds.

As soon as the guard was out of sight, the White Rabbit tapped twice on the wall.

A hedgehog popped up out of the dirt. "You all set?"

The White Rabbit nodded.

The first hedgehog and another one emerged from their burrow, allowing the White Rabbit and me to use the burrow to wriggle through to the other side of the wall. Spotting a patch of pink four-leaf clovers, I grabbed a handful.

"We must hurry," the White Rabbit whispered.

We crept along the wall until we got to the edge of the wood.

"Run." The White Rabbit sprinted into the forest.

I raced after him, but I soon had to stop and catch my breath. "Where are you taking me?"

"To Bill's cave. Come on. We're far enough away from the castle that we can walk now."

"Did you say Bill's cave?" I frowned. "I know for a fact that Bill doesn't trust you. He said you were a bully to him when he worked for you. I doubt he'd be doing you any favors."

"Bill and I have worked out our differences. I apologized for my behavior of the past and told him I'm not the same person I was then."

"Fair enough. So, who are you?"

Sighing, he said, "We're wasting valuable time—time the Gryphon can't afford to have us lose." He went on ahead.

As if I'd made the thing appear by thinking about it earlier, the Monarch Butterfly appeared and lit on my shoulder.

"Poor Alice. How much you've been through today," the Butterfly said. "You're exhausted. You aren't even sure you can carry on."

I staggered. "I didn't realize I *was* so tired."

"This adventure has taken a toll on you—that's for certain. You deserve a little rest. Only a minute." The Butterfly fluttered around my face.

"Only a minute," I agreed, sitting down at the base of a tree.

"What are you doing?" The White Rabbit came back to get me.

"I need a minute, that's all." I let my eyes drift shut.

"That's it," the Butterfly intoned. "Sleep, sweet Alice. A nap will do you a world of good."

"Get out of here!"

The White Rabbit was arguing with the Butterfly. I could hear them both, but I couldn't make out anything either of them was saying. Their voices were like the buzzing of honeybees.

Then the White Rabbit was shaking my shoulders. "Snap out of it!"

I shook off the trance I'd fallen into and got to my feet. "I'm sorry. Let's go."

"Never entertain that wicked butterfly even for a moment," he said.

"Is it a silverfish?"

"I don't know what it is, but it wants to trap you here. Constantly be on your guard, Gia."

CHAPTER 17

I felt weak and stupid after falling for the Butterfly's manipulation. The White Rabbit didn't chide me anymore, but I was doing so much self-flagellation that it might have been better if he had.

He led me to the mouth of a cave. "In here."

The cave looked dark and intimidating. "Matthew is here?"

"Yes."

I crept inside and found that the cave opened up into something more like a home than I would have ever imagined. The cobblestone floor was pierced in places by plants and dotted sporadically by moss. There was a stairway leading to a second tier of the cave, and small holes let in light from above.

"This looks like somewhere a Hobbit might live," I murmured.

"What is a Hobbit?" Bill asked.

I started at the sound of his voice, unaware he'd been close by. "A charming creature."

"Then I thank you." Bill gave a slight bow. "The Gryphon is this way."

He escorted the White Rabbit and me through a passage between two tree trunks. There was a squirrel on one of them, but it paid no attention to us.

Bill allowed me to go into the room first. The Gryphon was lying on an enormous basket filled with straw and blankets.

Running to his side, I ran my hand gently over his head. "I'm sorry I let this happen to you."

The Gryphon opened his eyes. "You couldn't have stopped it, sweetheart. I'm glad you escaped the King."

"That's all thanks to the White Rabbit. Here—these are supposed to have incredible healing properties." I gave him the pink four-leaf clovers.

"How do you know?" He examined one of the clovers skeptically.

"I read it in a book I found in the White Rabbit's house. I have it here." I took the book from my pocket and showed it to him. "I can't say for sure that this manuscript hasn't also been corrupted by the silverfish, but...."

He popped one into his mouth. "It tastes like honey. Thank you. Keep the rest until we see what effect this one has."

"All right." I happened to remember Lorina. "Bill, my

sister said she would look for the Gryphon. Have you seen her anywhere?"

"I don't think so." He rubbed his chin. "At least, I haven't seen anyone resembling you."

"We have to get these two out of here," the White Rabbit said. "The Gryphon is hurt, and Alice is fleeing from the King, who has possibly already realized she is missing and sent guards to find her. Plus, Alice is exhausted and very nearly succumbed to the Monarch Butterfly's enchantment."

"But where can we go?" I asked. "It seems to me that if Bill will have us, his cave is the safest place for us to be right now."

"I was thinking more of North Carolina," the White Rabbit said.

My jaw dropped. "Cooper?"

He nodded.

With a squeal of delight, I raced over, picked him up, and hugged him. "I can't tell you how relieved I am that you're okay!"

I heard the Gryphon chuckle, but then he grunted in pain. Putting the White Rabbit back down—he *was* my boss, no matter how cute and cuddly he looked at the moment, after all—I hurried back to the Gryphon's side.

"How badly are you hurt?" I asked.

"I'll be fine."

I wondered how long it would take the clovers to kick in and heal the Gryphon. The mushroom's effects had been instantaneous, but the clovers hadn't appeared to be working yet. Maybe the book couldn't be trusted. Maybe I'd given Matthew something that would cause him more harm than good.

"He'll be all right as soon as we get him back home," the White Rabbit said.

"How are you here?" I knew Cooper was not supposed to be in Literatia. His being here was in violation of some sort of peace treaty if I wasn't mistaken.

"I couldn't risk the two of you dying in this book! But we have no time for explanations." The White Rabbit consulted the watch in his waistcoat pocket, saw that—like every other clock in Wonderland—it had stopped working, and flung it down. "I know of a portal nearby. Leaving Wonderland is the only way to make sure the two of you will live."

"Where is North Carolina?" Bill asked.

"It's…um…" The White Rabbit sighed.

Seeing how the White Rabbit had no patience for Bill's question at the moment, I said, "It's a magical place with a fantastic library."

Bill gasped. "I would love to see this library."

The White Rabbit pinned me with a sardonic glare that clearly said, *Thanks a lot.*

I turned my attention back to the Gryphon. "I agree with the White Rabbit. We need to go to the portal."

He nodded. "Help me up."

With Bill and the White Rabbit on one side and me on the other, we managed to get the Gryphon to his feet.

He wobbled momentarily, but then he said, "I've got this."

Bill stepped back, but the White Rabbit and I did not. We understood the urgency of getting the Gryphon to the portal as soon as possible.

We managed to get the Gryphon into the foyer, but before we could leave the cave, we heard something at the mouth of the cave. My hand tightened on the Gryphon's shoulder as I looked around to see what I could use as a weapon.

A single soldier ventured into the cave. It was the Seven of Hearts.

Bill stepped to the front of the group. "Seven, what are you doing here?"

"I mean no one any harm," Seven said. "In fact, I'm here because I heard you trying to convince the King of Alice's innocence. I also believe she is innocent."

"You do?" I asked.

"Yes. Before the Queen went missing, I saw her arguing with someone near the garden gate. They walked out together, and then—"

We heard a *whoosh* as Seven abruptly stopped speaking, and then we watched in horror as a small flame began to spread over him. Bill and the White Rabbit rushed forward. The White Rabbit knocked Seven to the ground, and Bill threw a rug over him to smother the fire. Unfortunately, they were too late. When Bill lifted the rug, Seven was practically a pile of ash. A burnt match was to Seven's left.

Bill raced from the cave.

"Someone shot him with a flaming match," I said. "Who would do that?"

In unspoken agreement, we waited for Bill to return before attempting to leave. We had no idea who else might be outside.

When he returned just a few minutes later, Bill was furious, and his face was streaked with tears. "Seven was a good soldier and an even better friend. He was killed because he knows who slew the Queen. I won't rest until Seven's killer is caught and punished."

"Did you see anyone or anything outside?" the White Rabbit asked.

"Nothing, but I'm going back outside to see if I can find anyone lurking around."

"Thank you for your hospitality," the Gryphon said. "We are going to the portal now."

"I'm glad I could help you." Bill gave us a nod and then bounded back outside.

The White Rabbit assessed the Gryphon warily. "I know traveling will be difficult for you, but we have no choice."

"I'm okay."

We regarded him skeptically.

"Seriously, I'm beginning to feel better," he said. "Let's get to that portal."

"Everyone be extra cautious," the White Rabbit said. "These soldiers may be merely playing cards in our eyes, but here in Wonderland, they're much more than that."

"Yes, and the injuries they inflict are real." The Gryphon tried to manage a smile, but he couldn't quite pull it off. "Besides that, there's an enemy in the forest who won't hesitate to cut down anyone who comes close to solving the mystery of the Queen's murder."

***

WE WERE WALKING SLOWER and more cautiously than any of us would have liked, but that couldn't be helped. Although I was alert to every sound, every scent, every glimpse of something different, my mind was flooded with questions.

Where had Bill gone? I wished we could have joined him in searching for Seven's assassin, but it was imperative that the White Rabbit and I get the Gryphon through the portal.

"Will you return to Bill's cave once you've guided us home?" I asked.

"That's the plan," the White Rabbit said. "Bill is a gentle soul. I don't believe he'll take vengeance on the murderer. Bill would prefer to see justice done and will take the culprit to the King."

"Seven's killer might have merely been another soldier sent by the King," the Gryphon said. "After all, the King had the most to gain from the Queen's death."

"Maybe not," I said. "He always had more power than the Queen. He was simply too weak or too indulgent to exercise that power. He could have exerted himself at any time."

"That's an excellent point," the Gryphon said. "But if not the King, then who?"

"With the manuscript so damaged, it could be almost anyone—a wronged soldier, a flamingo who was tired of being used as a croquet mallet." I paused. "But I feel that the manner in which the Queen was murdered points to a human, and the Cook acted strangely from the moment we met her. First, she and the Duchess moved the Queen into the Duchess's house, and then she managed to get the Queen back to the castle."

"True," the White Rabbit said, "but if the Cook committed the crime, then she's working with someone else. She couldn't do all those things alone."

The Gryphon grunted in pain but quickly spoke to try to mask his discomfort. "Do you think it's the Duchess who was working with the Cook?"

"Possibly, but I find that unlikely. The—" The White Rabbit stopped, his ears twitching as he heard something moving ahead of us. "Don't move."

CHAPTER 18

I released the breath I'd been holding as a large puppy scampered into our path. In *Alice's Adventures in Wonderland*, shrunken Alice had encountered an "enormous puppy." And although the puppy wanted to play with Alice, she was terrified that it would trample her.

This puppy wasn't too large for normal-sized Alice to handle.

Smiling, I said, "Hi, there."

"Hello." It lifted its nose and morphed from a puppy into something much larger. "I smell blood. Here we have an injured Gryphon, a tasty old rabbit, a feeble little girl, and a hungry beast."

Gasping, I took a step backward.

The Beast bared its fangs. They were dripping with saliva, and there were silverfish crawling all over them. As its hackles rose, the Gryphon put himself between it and the rest of us.

"I won't be as easy to break apart as Edith was," the Beast said, as it sidestepped the Gryphon and lunged at me.

Although I dodged, the Beast was quick, and it clamped down on my arm. I screamed in pain and kicked at the Beast, but I was unable to make it let me go. This creature was more powerful and vicious than Edith could have ever hoped to be.

The White Rabbit leapt on the Beast, pulling its tail and biting its legs.

Seemingly annoyed by the interruption, the Beast let go of me and turned its attention to the White Rabbit. "Stay out of this, old man."

Old man? Did the Beast know that the White Rabbit was Cooper?

Shrieking, I watched in horror as the Beast grasped the White Rabbit in his mouth and slung him several feet away.

With a guttural roar, the Gryphon once again put himself directly in front of the Beast. The Beast sprang at the Gryphon's throat. The Gryphon was able to parry the attack using his good wing and talons, and he threw the Beast off him.

The Beast attacked the Gryphon again, biting the Gryphon's neck and drawing blood.

Not seeing any other weapon, I wrenched a stick off of a nearby tree. I beat the Beast on the head while the White Rabbit also ran to assist the Gryphon.

The Beast turned loose of the Gryphon long enough

to snarl and snap at me. I refused to let it faze me, as I batted the mass of silverfish as hard as I could. If I'd caused Edith to disintegrate, surely I could at least do enough damage to this creature to keep it from killing one or all of us.

Withstanding my blows, the Beast hurled itself at my face. I felt its hot breath on me and smelled the blood on its breath as it lowered its head. I tried to jab the stick between us, but I couldn't.

The Gryphon dived onto the Beast's back and bit its shoulder. Howling, the Beast tried to shake off the Gryphon as I resumed striking the Beast with the stick. The Beast collapsed beneath the Gryphon.

When the Gryphon moved off the Beast, the Beast crawled a short distance away. The Gryphon, the White Rabbit, and I prepared for another attack, but it didn't come.

Bill ran among us, brandishing a flaming torch. "Get up and get out of here, you vile creature, before I finish you off!"

The Beast rose on unsteady legs. "You might have won this battle, but you have many still to fight." He limped away.

Blowing out the flame, Bill asked, "Is everyone all right?"

Ignoring his question, I asked one of my own. "How did you do that? Can you breathe fire?"

"Sadly, no. I found these matches discarded in the forest," he said. "When I heard you scream, I abandoned the search for Seven's killer and came to help. In fact, I thought you might be fighting with Seven's assailant, but I don't think so now."

"Neither do we," the White Rabbit said. "We appreciate your help."

"What *was* that creature?" Bill asked. "I've never seen anything like it."

The White Rabbit, the Gryphon, and I searched each other's faces for something reasonable to tell Bill. We couldn't tell him the truth—that he was in a book damaged extensively by silverfish and that only by solving the Queen's murder could we reset the book to its original state and save the manuscript from disappearing as if it had never been written in the first place. Besides that, Bill might not *want* the manuscript to revert to its original state. He'd been a lizard before, and now he was a dragon.

"It's apparent that many strange and frightening things are happening in Wonderland," the Gryphon said. "First, the Queen is murdered, then Seven is struck down, and now this bloodthirsty creature shows up."

"I don't know what to make of any of it," Bill said. "Wonderland hasn't always been a carefree world, but it wasn't dangerous—not even when the Queen was threatening to have everyone executed."

"Hopefully, we can all work together to restore Wonderland to its former condition," the White Rabbit said.

KEEPING a watchful eye out for the Beast and any other predators, we continued on our trek toward the portal.

"Where are we going again?" Bill asked.

"Alice and the Gryphon have suffered greatly in their struggle to reclaim Wonderland from villains like the Beast," the White Rabbit said. "I know of a place where I can hide them until they can recuperate. Then, if you'd be so kind, perhaps you can help me put Wonderland right again."

Bowing his head slightly, Bill said, "I would be honored."

Bill droned on about never daring to dream that one day he'd be a hero to all of Wonderland; and although I smiled and nodded every so often, I tuned him out. I was concentrating on who could possibly need matches in Wonderland.

It was never nighttime in this book, so no one would require a candle, except maybe in the dungeon. I felt fortunate that the White Rabbit had the foresight to bring a flashlight when he'd come to Literatia to rescue me.

Had he come for the purpose of rescuing me? Not likely. Which was fine. If he'd read that the soldiers had shot down the Gryphon—the manuscript changed with every new thing that happened until it was finally reset— then the White Rabbit would have been desperate to save his father. I, too, was anxious about the Gryphon and wanted him out of this book as soon as possible. I clenched my fists and winced from the pain of the bite on my arm.

This could be fun, I'd thought when I'd found myself in *Alice's Adventures in Wonderland*. All the fascinating characters, the tiny cakes labeled *eat me* and bottles instructing Alice to *drink me*. I had sorely underestimated this place and all the risks it posed.

I hadn't realized I'd dropped back from the group until the Gryphon joined me.

"Are you all right?" he asked.

"Yes. I'm trying to determine who here would have matches. The soldiers who guard the dungeon might, although Two didn't carry a lamp or a candlestick. Come to think of it, I didn't see anyone in the dungeon with a lantern. The only other character here who might have a match is the Cook."

"Good point," he said. "Now tell me what you're *really* thinking."

"That *is* what I'm thinking. I want to solve this murder so we—or at least one or two of us—can go home." I sighed. "I don't even care if I don't go home. I just can hardly wait to leave this crazy, mixed-up world where playing cards run the show and can throw you in prison for...well, forever."

"You *will* get to go home, Gia." His voice was barely above a whisper. "I promise. As soon as we get to that portal, you're going home."

"Only if you come with me," I said.

Reader, I had no intention of going through that portal. You likely believe me to be a horrible liar who is lower than a worm's belly; but trust me, you aren't calling me any names I wasn't calling myself.

Matthew was badly injured. I was a little worse for wear, but I wasn't seriously hurt like he was. My plan was to either push him or trick him into going through the portal ahead of me and then slamming the door shut...if there *was* a door.

Cooper, who was some sort of magical prodigy, wasn't even supposed to be in Literatia. The Wellinghams had made that agreement with the silverfish decades ago. When he was a child, the Council of the Silverfish wanted to destroy Cooper. His parents had tried their best to keep Cooper out of Literatia ever since.

His mother, who had been the curator of Smithmore Manor Library, turned the job over to Cooper before she died. Matthew agreed to be imprisoned in Literatia to assure the council that the Wellinghams wouldn't allow Cooper to come into their world and completely destroy them. Matthew's voluntary entrapment in the book world had been part of their peace treaty.

In order to save Matthew and me, Cooper had breached the treaty. If two of us were going to go through that portal to the safety of Smithmore Manor, I had every intention of it being Matthew and Cooper.

CHAPTER 19

The tree the White Rabbit had been searching for was massive. Its trunk was at least the circumference of a tractor tire, and its leafy branches spread out fifty yards in all directions.

"It's amazing." I touched the bark lightly.

"Careful." The White Rabbit lifted both his gloved paws, splayed them on the trunk, and began feeling all around. After circling the entire tree, he said, "It's not here."

"The portal?" the Gryphon asked.

"Yes. It was supposed to be here, but it isn't."

"Maybe it's up higher than you thought. I'll lift you up." The Gryphon lifted the White Rabbit, and they began another trip around the tree.

Bill shrugged at me, and I shrugged back. He and I were merely observers at this point, waiting to see what would happen next.

When they circled back to us, the Gryphon placed the White Rabbit gently on the ground.

"It's not here," the White Rabbit repeated, his voice ending in a sigh.

"Then we have no other choice," I said. "You two accompany Bill back to his cave and stay there with him until I discover who killed the Queen."

"Not happening," the Gryphon said.

"Agreed." The White Rabbit scanned the perimeter. "The Beast is still out there somewhere and would love to catch you alone."

"As is whoever killed poor Seven," Bill added.

"I can handle myself." I straightened my back and lifted my chin, realizing as I did so that I was still in a little girl's body and could draw myself up only so much. Still, I wasn't backing down from my position.

"I could go with you." Bill's expression was earnest, but if he *could* be trusted, I'd rather he stayed with the Gryphon and the White Rabbit.

Squinting as a twitching tail materialized, I asked, "Vidocq?"

"*Oui.*" He became completely visible. "What have I missed?"

We quickly updated him on what had happened since we saw him last.

"How did the assassin kill the soldier with the match?" Vidocq asked. "Was it thrown like the javelin? Shot, as from the sling?"

"I felt that it was shot," the Gryphon answered. "It was

projected so forcefully that I believe it pierced the… um…" He had been about to say either *card* or *cardboard* but stopped in deference to Bill. "I'm not sure the match could've been thrown that hard."

Vidocq nodded. "Interesting."

"Since we were unable to find the portal, I feel our best solution is solve the Queen's murder so that—" I, too, was mindful of Bill and his confusion about how his world—bizarre though it was—was changing. "So that everything will return to normal. Bill, would you please stay with the Gryphon and the White Rabbit while the Cheshire Cat and I find the killer?"

"I will do whatever you ask of me in order to bring Seven's killer to justice," he said.

"Alice, I'm insulted that you find me weak and help-less," the White Rabbit said. "Have you never heard the old adage about great things coming in small packages?"

"I have, and you're extremely valuable indeed," I said. "That's why you must be protected."

"It's imperative to me that you stay with the Gryphon and allow me to take the lead in this investigation." The White Rabbit's eyes bore into mine, and the guise fell away momentarily, allowing me to see the man rather than the illusion.

"This arguing is most unproductive," Vidocq said. "If it's a portal you wish to find, then we must return to the rabbit hole."

Shaking my head, I said, "The rabbit hole might lead

us out of Wonderland, but would it lead us where we need to go?"

"Perhaps not the rabbit hole itself, but one of the many doors within it could very well open onto the portal." Vidocq inclined his head. "Since the silverfish corruption of the manuscript—I mean, of Wonderland— led to the portal not being where the White Rabbit had believed it to be, it stands to reason that the portal would be hidden in the most logical place, *non?*"

"Nothing in Wonderland is logical," I said.

"Which is why that's where the portal should be." Vidocq winked.

I tried to break down Vidocq's thought process. Since everything in Wonderland was illogical, the fact that the portal would be found somewhere logical was unreasonable and, therefore, the most likely place it would be.

Apparently, the Gryphon grasped the idea before I did. "That's an excellent theory."

"*Merci.*" Vidocq grinned like the Cheshire Cat he was.

"And how do we go about locating the rabbit hole?" the White Rabbit asked.

"I'd have thought you'd know that better than anyone," Bill said.

The White Rabbit looked annoyed but didn't respond.

I removed the book from my pocket and handed it to the White Rabbit. "Maybe this will help. Chapter one is all about maps and secret passages."

The rabbit opened the book and quickly scanned the

first chapter. "It says here that the rabbit hole is at the front right corner of the garden."

"That makes sense. It was in the rabbit hole that Alice first discovered the garden," the Gryphon said.

"Correct." Vidocq nodded. "She was either too big or needed a key or something, but we know she could see the garden from the rabbit hole."

"It's too dangerous for Alice to be near the garden." The White Rabbit's nose twitched. "The King will most likely be searching for her to toss her back into the dungeon by now."

"Then maybe the Cheshire Cat and I could draw the soldiers' fire, so to speak, by allowing them to think they've trapped me." I glanced at Vidocq to make sure he'd go along with my plan, but I was unable to read his expression. "That way, the White Rabbit, the Gryphon, and Bill can locate the portal."

"There is absolutely no way you're going to be bait for the King," the Gryphon said. "You've managed to escape him once. This time, he might instruct his soldiers to shoot you on sight."

"As is the usual state of affairs, I shall be the hero."

I rolled my eyes at Vidocq's arrogance, and he hissed at me.

"Sorry." I wasn't really.

"As I was saying," he went on, "our best—*non*, our *only* —solution is for me to go to the garden and distract the guards so that you may locate and make use of the portal while I solve the Queen's murder and set all things right once more."

"I will help you, Mr. Cat." Bill appeared eager to help in whatever capacity he could.

"That does sound like a reasonable solution," I said, knowing I was planning—and that I wasn't likely the only one—to stay behind and help Vidocq.

To the extent possible, we stayed hidden in the forest as we trekked back to the garden. We were all on the lookout for the Beast and anything else suspicious, and I was still hoping to catch a glimpse of the Blue Caterpillar. It might be unwise to eat anymore of the Caterpillar's magic mushrooms, but I held firm to the belief that my being a giant could go a long way in helping us out of our current predicament.

Hearing someone coming up fast behind us, I looked around for some sort of weapon as I turned. The Gryphon got in front of me, and Bill jumped ahead of all of us.

It was the Cook. As usual, she was carrying a pot, but she wasn't brandishing it as a weapon.

"Who are you and what do you want?" Bill demanded.

"You know good and well who I am." The Cook glared at him.

"Did you kill Seven?" he asked.

"Seven what?" She frowned.

"The soldier—my friend."

"I don't know what you're talking about." She looked beyond Bill to me. "I have to return to the Duchess's house, but I was compelled to come and tell you to beware the King."

"You're a little late." I told her about being imprisoned for the Queen's death. "Did the King kill the Queen?"

"Here's all I know. Soldiers brought the Queen to the Duchess's house and told us that she would be staying there," the Cook said. "They later came back and got her, saying they were taking her to the castle, but the Duchess and I were not to say anything to anyone about her besides that the Queen was resting."

"Why are you confiding in us now?" the Gryphon asked.

"Because the Pig told me to."

When Alice had first entered the Duchess's house in *Alice's Adventures in Wonderland*, the Duchess had been holding a baby that later turned into a pig while Alice was holding it. That must be the pig to which the Cook referred. But who was this pig to us, and why did it want us to know that the King was responsible for hiding the Queen at the Duchess's house?

"My duty is done," the Cook said, hurrying back in the direction from whence she'd come.

"That was weird," the White Rabbit said.

"It was," I agreed. "Do we believe her?"

Vidocq nodded. "I do. Why would she lie? She didn't

tell us who killed the Queen, only that the King requested that she be hidden."

"That means that whoever killed the Queen didn't care if she were found," I said. "The King's request that she be hidden means that he knew she was dead before he ever accepted my invitation to follow me into the clearing to find her."

"Curiouser and curiouser," Vidocq mumbled.

CHAPTER 20

From the forest, we watched the sentries patrolling the garden with their weird, wobbly walks.

"Stay out of sight while I locate the rabbit hole," the White Rabbit said.

As Vidocq and Bill observed the White Rabbit racing toward the garden, I pulled the Gryphon aside so the two of us could speak privately.

"It's really important to me that you and the White Rabbit are the ones going through the portal," I said. "The two of you have had so little time together. You've missed so much of your son's life. I refuse to keep you apart any longer."

"You didn't sign up for banishment to Literatia when you took the job at Smithmore Manor."

I shrugged. "That's true. In fact, I never even knew traveling through a portal into a book world was possible until my first day on the job." I smiled. "But this is my life now. You—all of you, even Vidocq—are my family now. And I can give you time with your son. Let me do that for you. For both of you."

The Gryphon hugged me. "My deepest wish is that we could all be together at home in North Carolina."

"That's my wish too, but we both know that isn't possible because of the treaty between the silverfish and the Wellinghams."

"The silverfish have violated it multiple times, as you well know," he said. "And Cooper breached it when he became the White Rabbit to help us. I'm confident I can find a way to get all of us home where we belong. Together."

"I pray that you're right, but please take the White Rabbit and go through the portal as soon as possible. I'm afraid that if you don't, one or both of you will die."

"That's exactly what I'm afraid will happen to you." He stepped back so he could examine my face. "I won't let anything happen to you."

"I'm close to solving the mystery of the Queen's murder and resetting the book. I can feel it."

He opened his mouth to speak again, but Vidocq called to us.

"Hurry, *mes amis*! The White Rabbit has found the rabbit hole."

The Gryphon, Bill, Vidocq, and I ran out of the forest to the edge of the garden where we crouched down behind the white board fence.

The White Rabbit moved aside to show us a burrow

that appeared to be much too small to accommodate a rabbit, much less all of us. "Here's the rabbit hole. All we need to do is determine which of the many doors inside leads to the portal. Let's go."

As he disappeared into the opening, the Gryphon and I looked at each other.

"I'm not sure I'll fit," I said.

"There's only one way to find out," he said.

"Perhaps Bill and I should remain behind and act as the lookouts." Vidocq winked at me.

He knew that neither he nor Bill could go through the portal and was lagging behind to protect Bill's feelings.

I kissed his cheek. "You're truly a wonderful friend."

Grinning, he said, "I know."

"Thank you, Bill," I said. "You're a hero."

"I appreciate your kind words," he said.

With a deep breath and a look of apprehension at the Gryphon, I stuck the toe of my shoe into the hole. It opened to accommodate the rest of me, and I went through without any trouble whatsoever.

The White Rabbit was waiting for me. "What took you so long?"

"I was worried I wouldn't fit."

Seeing how easily I'd made it down the rabbit hole encouraged the Gryphon, and he was there within seconds of my arrival. "That wasn't so bad."

"Here comes the fun part," the White Rabbit said. "We must open each of these doors until we find the portal. The easiest way to accomplish this will be to split up.

Beware of whatever you find lurking behind the doors. If it isn't the portal, the wisest thing you can do is shut the door and move on. Understood?"

Reader, he was peering into my eyes as if he could read my mind.

"Of course," I said. "When we find the portal, how will we let the others know?"

"Yell," he said. "At that point, we won't care if anyone overhears us."

THE FIRST DOOR I opened led to a shadow world. Everything was literally a silhouette. I slammed that one shut pretty quickly. Wonderland was spooky enough in perpetual daylight.

The second door was golden and glittery and, quite frankly, looked like it would be the perfect type of door for a portal to be behind. Unless, of course, it was designed to trick me.

I turned the knob and stuck my head inside far enough to see what was in the room. There wasn't a portal, but there was a blue rug and a large control panel. As I eased closer to read the dials on the control panel, the door slammed shut behind me.

Gulping, I decided to figure out what the contraption did before seeing whether or not I could get out of the room. No need to panic just yet.

The dials were *DAY, DATE,* and *YEAR.*

I could visit the past.

Looking over my shoulder to make sure the White Rabbit wasn't bursting into the room and shouting at me for disobeying his orders, I stepped onto the blue rug.

Mom and I had always loved Saturdays. It was our special day, and we'd always do something fun.

Stretching my hand out toward the *YEAR* dial, I hesitated. What if I went back and couldn't return to the present? What if I remained teenaged Gia stuck in a single Saturday with Mom forever? Of course, that would mean Mom wouldn't be ravaged by cancer and die.

Wait, what was I doing? I couldn't just drop everything and galivant off into the past. What if something terrible happened to Matthew and Cooper while I was gone? Or what if I couldn't get back?

"What are you waiting for?"

I started at the whisper that came from my left side.

It was the Butterfly.

Shaking my head, I said, "No. I'm not going."

"Why not?"

"I need to help the Gryphon and the White Rabbit. They're counting on me."

"I understand." The Butterfly fluttered near my cheek. "Still, it would be wonderful to see your mother one last time, wouldn't it?"

"How do you even *know* where I considered going?"

"It's not hard to imagine. Your mother's death was not so long ago, and she was still young. Why not take the opportunity to see her one last time? You won't miss anything here. You *know* how much more slowly time passes in Literatia."

"What if I get stuck there?" I narrowed my eyes. "You'd like that, wouldn't you?"

"I would. But there's a time limit on the machine. You can't stay there for more than the specified date."

I stepped closer to examine the machine, my feet still on the blue rug. I knew the Butterfly was manipulative, but could the creature be telling me the truth? Would I be able to return?

At the end, I wasn't even sure Mom had known who I was anymore. I could go back and talk with her one last time, and then I could return to Literatia, solve the Queen's murder, and reset *Alice's Adventures in Wonderland*.

"One last chat...the two of you healthy and happy. You could tell her anything you'd neglected to say before."

"Hush. I—"

The Butterfly interrupted. "You'll never get an opportunity like this again."

Surely, I could get back. If there was a way in, there was certainly a way out. I reached for the dial again, and this time I turned it quickly—before I could change my mind.

As soon as I'd put in the day and the date, the room began to spin. I wished there was something I could cling to in order to keep from getting dizzy and falling. Instead, I simply closed my eyes.

The room stopped spinning, and I opened my eyes. I was standing in my half of the bedroom I'd shared with Mom. She'd put curtains up to divide the room so I'd have the illusion of having my own room, but a one-bedroom apartment was all we could afford.

Taking a deep breath, I could smell pancake batter infused with vanilla and a hint of cinnamon. Smiling, I strode to the kitchen.

There was Mom with her hair piled on top of her head in a messy bun. She was wearing jeans, a sweatshirt, and fuzzy pink slippers. I hugged her from behind.

"What are you doing?" She laughed. "You're gonna make me burn the pancakes."

"I don't even care."

"You'll care when you're eating burned pancakes."

I held her a moment longer before letting her go. "I love you, you know."

"I love you, too." She paused. "Wait a minute. What do you want?"

It was my turn to laugh. "Nothing."

She glanced at me over her shoulder and arched a brow.

"Seriously," I said, "I just wanted you to know how much I appreciate you."

"Oh, my goodness." She shook her head. "It's something so big that you're afraid to come right out and ask me."

I got plates and cups out of the cabinet and set the table. As I was retrieving the silverware, there was a knock on the door.

Mom's smile morphed into a grimace, and she rubbed her head. "Gia, could you please take over for me?"

"Sure." I closed the silverware drawer and went over to the stove.

She grabbed her wallet on the way to the door, and it dawned on me that it was the first of the month. The rent was due.

Flipping the pancakes, I heard Mom quietly begging Mr. Turner for more time.

"I promise I'll have the rest of it to you by the end of next week."

"We go through this every month," Mr. Turner said. "I can't keep carrying you. You're either going have to start paying on time or get out."

"I know. I'm so sorry."

"She's doing the best she can," I said loudly.

Mom looked mortified.

"Aren't we all?" Mr. Turner took the money Mom had given him and walked away.

"You shouldn't have said that," she said, returning to the stove and taking back over the pancake production.

"Why not? It's true."

"Well, he's doing the best he can too." She nodded toward the window.

I peered out and saw a medical supply delivery truck outside the apartment building. "What's that?"

"They're bringing a hospital bed and some supplies for Mrs. Turner. She doesn't have much longer."

"Oh. I never knew…." I rubbed the goosebumps that had raised on my arms. Within a few years, it would be Mom with the hospital bed, and I'd be the one at the end of her rope. Poor Mr. Turner. I wish I'd known and been kinder to him.

A butterfly flew through the room. It was a beautiful purple monarch butterfly. It landed on my shoulder.

"You *can* be kinder to Mr. Turner. And kinder to your mother. You were never this nice to her on Saturday mornings."

"I was too!"

The butterfly took flight.

"You were what?" Mom asked. "And hand me a plate to put these pancakes on."

I took a plate over to the stove. "I was kind to you, wasn't I?"

"Yes." She drew out the word. "You are being *very* weird this morning."

"I'm not supposed to be here."

"Where are you supposed to be?" she asked.

The butterfly lit on my mother's back. "Here," it whispered. "You need to stay here."

"I love you, Mom, but there's something I need to take care of." I hurried into the bedroom and stepped onto the blue rug. The room began to spin, and I closed my eyes.

As soon as I opened my eyes in the room to the past, I

hurried out and shut the door firmly behind me. I was almost afraid to open another door after that.

The next door was pink and white. I flung it wide, as if I were ripping off a bandage. Inside was a table of treats: tiny cakes with *Eat Me* piped on top in icing calligraphy, bottles embellished with *Drink Me*, and mushrooms. The mushrooms looked exactly like the ones that had made me shrink and grow.

I knew it wasn't wise, but I ran into the room and stuffed my pockets with those mushrooms. I'd only use them in case of an emergency, but I'd looked for them too hard to ignore them when they were right in front of me.

Rushing back out into the hallway, I closed the door and opened the next. This one was blue, and inside the room was nothing but a pedestal holding a large book. Curiosity got the best of me, and I crept toward the book.

Curiosity got the best of Alice, and she crept toward the book.

Those words wrote themselves across the page as I watched. I gasped.

Alice gasped.

This was *my* story. I could use it to find out who killed the Queen. I tried to turn back the pages.

Thinking she could use the book to determine who killed the Queen, Alice tried to turn back the pages. Silly Alice! That isn't how books work. Books need to be read from beginning to end. Afterward, one may reread them, but one can't simply turn pages willy-nilly. The story won't make sense.

"I don't need it to make sense," I muttered. "I need to know who killed the Queen!"

Alice was so distraught that she was talking to herself. Poor dear! Didn't she realize what would happen to her if she continued to disobey the law of books? Apparently not. She should lift her eyes to the ceiling.

Doing as the book instructed, I raised my eyes and saw an axe hanging above my head. Every time I tried to turn the page, the axe dropped a little lower.

With a squeal of terror, I sprinted out of the room and right into Lorina.

CHAPTER 21

"Lorina! What are you doing here in the rabbit hole?"

"Searching for you," she said.

"Edith told me earlier that you'd been arrested by the King's guards," I said. "Was that a lie, or did you manage to escape the dungeon?"

"It was a lie." Lorina shook her head. "I told you already, Edith is quite different from you and me. I've been all over Wonderland hunting for you. Where have you been?"

"I actually *was* captured and thrown in the dungeon, but I managed to escape with the help of a friend."

"You must've been so frightened." Lorina hugged me, and she smelled like lavender. "I'm here now, and I'll keep you safe. Let's get out of this rabbit hole. It's making me feel claustrophobic."

"Go on ahead, and I'll be out soon. I can't leave my friends. They need my help to find something."

"All you have to do to escape this place is wake up, Alice."

"But I am awake," I said.

"You only think you're awake. In truth, you're still with me on the riverbank. If I can't rouse you out of this dream soon, you'll never be the same."

Frowning, I asked, "What do you mean?"

She stretched out her hand and brushed the hair back from my face, and I spotted a rubber band encircling her wrist.

"What's that?" I pointed at the band.

Glancing at it, she answered, "It's a rubber band."

"Where did you get it?"

"It was around a bundle of papers on Papa's desk. I'll put it back when we get home."

I was quiet, remembering the flaming match that came flying at Seven. Had it been propelled into the card by a rubber band?

"Alice, please wake up!"

"Why?" Having the sudden urge to make myself gigantic, I put my hand in my pocket and closed it over the mushrooms I'd taken earlier. I wasn't going to eat one yet, but knowing it was there made me feel less afraid.

"Because this dream is taking you away from me. It's underscoring the fact that you're growing up. And so am I. Soon you won't need me anymore."

"I'll always need my sister."

"You won't," she said. "It won't be long before we're both married and have households of our own to run.

Who knows how far we'll end up from each other? We might go months or even years without seeing each other."

"No matter how busy our lives get, we'll always be close." I was trying to soothe her and still work out whether or not she'd killed the Queen and Seven. "If we can't see each other, we can at least write."

Lorina grunted in frustration. "You're doing it already!"

"Doing what?"

"Pulling away from me. This place has ruined you. I hate it!"

"Did you shoot Seven with a flaming match?" I asked.

Her eyes bore into mine. "Yes! He saw me arguing with that stupid Queen. I told her to let you *play*—to have a tea party, to enjoy a game of croquet, to have a little fun without some power-mad matriarch screaming orders to chop off your head."

She gave up fighting back tears and let them flow. I released the mushroom and took my hand from my pocket.

"When you fell asleep, I realized your dream had become a nightmare," she said. "I came to save you. Wonderland could have been a lovely place for you to dream. Instead, it's horrible."

"Why didn't you want Seven to tell us you'd argued with the Queen?" I asked.

"I knew you'd be angry to learn that I'm the one who ripped her head off."

I patted her shoulder. "I'm not angry. But I would like to know why you did it."

"She was so overbearing! I got sick of her shouting, *off with her head!* or *off with his head!* every few minutes. Well, Queen, off with *your* head—how about that?"

"But, Lorina, she never did it."

"So what? She was a playing card, for crying out loud. The soldier was too. What difference did it make that a couple of them got destroyed?"

"It matters," I said. "Here in Wonderland, they're more than cards."

"The Queen was making you miserable. In fact, most of the creatures you met either quarreled with you or made you unhappy."

Rubbing my forehead, I said, "Learning how to deal with other people—without murdering them—is part of growing up."

"I don't want to grow up, and I don't want you to either."

"It's inevitable. Your killing the Queen and Seven didn't change that."

"I didn't *kill* anyone," Lorina said. "I tore up a couple of playing cards. Big deal."

"It is a big deal to those in Wonderland. And to me."

She scoffed. "No wonder. The Dodo created this place for you. You were the heroine. He relegated me to the role of the Lory, a dumb bird who did nothing but complain."

"I'm sure Mr. Dodgson didn't see you in that light." I

wondered why the book wasn't resetting. Lorina had confessed to me, and there really wasn't much to be done as far as meting out justice.

Maybe the book *was* resetting. It was possible that the Gryphon and the White Rabbit had found the portal, had gone through it, and that I was to remain in Wonderland until another assignment came along. I hoped it would be soon.

"He *did* see me in that light," Lorina said. "He, the stuttering Dodo, and I, the stupid Lory. I don't know what on earth would possess anyone to...."

While she was still talking, she began to fade, or else I did. Feeling dizzy, I closed my eyes and let the waves wash over me.

───────

I OPENED my eyes to see an unfamiliar—and yet, so very familiar—face. I smiled. "Matthew."

"I'm here, sweetheart."

Raising my hand, I touched his slightly stubbly cheek. "You're amazing."

"*You're* amazing."

Reader, he was gorgeous. It was as if someone had taken all of Edward Rochester's and Charles Darnay's best characteristics and combined them into this magnificent man. But what would he think of me?

"Am I what you expected?" I asked.

After all, Jane Eyre was a plain Jane, and Lucie

Manette Darnay was beautiful. Hopefully, I fell somewhere in between.

"Not at all." His lips formed into a slight smile. "You're
even better than I could have ever imagined."

I laughed, hoping he was telling me the truth. "I've
waited so long for this."

"So have I."

"Cooper offered to show me photos of you, but I
didn't want to see them until we could see each other
face to face," I said. "It didn't seem fair."

Now I wanted to go back and look at all the photos—
Matthew as a baby, every school year, even photographs
of him with Cooper and Cooper's mother. But there
would be time for that later.

"Where *is* Cooper?" I looked around the library.

Matthew sat with me on one of the brown leather
sofas and took both my hands in his. "Cooper stayed in
Literatia."

"How?" I nearly came up out of my seat. "I thought
the Council of the Silverfish had a bounty on him!"

"They did. But that was nearly half a century ago. He
doesn't think they would ever recognize him now, and I
tend to agree." He gazed down at our clasped hands.
"Cooper's health scare terrified me, and I think it rattled
him as well."

"Which is all the more reason the two of you should
be here together."

Bringing his eyes back up to mine, he said, "Perhaps,
but I see his point as well."

"What point?"

"As you know, time passes much more slowly in Literatia. He's well now and in great shape, especially for a man his age."

I nodded. "And he can remain that way for—what—forty years?"

"At least." He chuckled. "Plus, I think he was eager for the adventure. I'm sure we'll see him soon."

ALSO BY G. LEESON

Have you read the prequel to the series, SAVING PIGLET? If you haven't but would like to do so, please visit this link: https://dl.bookfunnel.com/4i9dt3pxir

ACKNOWLEDGMENTS

I'd like to thank my amazing beta readers (Rachel V., Valeri S., Lorraine O., and Debi P.) and Bethany P., who is fantastic help when it comes to brainstorming! I'd also like to give a shout-out to my wonderful family for believing in me even when I'm ready to give up writing altogether and go to work for Spirit Halloween (which I think would be really fun if I could just get paid for dressing up and playing with Halloween props). Last, but certainly not least, if you're looking for some amazing cover art, check out covervillain.com.

ABOUT THE AUTHOR

G. Leeson might appear to be new to writing, but she's better known as Gayle Leeson. As Gayle Leeson, she writes cozy mysteries; but a marketing expert warned her that cozy readers might not follow her into the portal fantasy realm. She, on the other hand, will read just about anything. If you'd like to see what else Gayle has written, please visit her website at https://www.gayleleeson.com/.

If you'd like to get an exclusive prequel to the series and learn how Cooper was introduced to Literatia, click here to read Saving Piglet.

EYRE OF MYSTERY
SNEAK PEEK

Have you read the first book in the Literatia series?
Here's a sneak peek at Chapter One of An Eyre of
Mystery.

CHAPTER 1

Chapter One

Where am I? These buildings...the streets—nothing looks normal. Nothing looks modern. And the smell. Ugh. It nearly made me gag. I looked down and saw I was standing beside a pile of fresh horse dung. The horse swished its tail as it passed.

"—goa raight to t' divil then!"

"Huh?" At the sound of the brusque female voice, I raised my chin. "Are you talking to me?"

She was. Or, rather, she had been. Now the forbidding old woman dressed like she'd just stepped out of a Brontë novel shook her head, put her nose in the air, and strode on. What was that she'd said? Was it even English?

Realizing my own clothes felt a bit strange, I glanced down at the fancy, floor-length skirt I was wearing. It was a dark red satin with white and gray stripes. I imagined the bonnet tied at my throat matched it.

Am I in costume? Maybe I was in a play. No. There wouldn't be real horse dung in a play. Besides, I wasn't on a stage.

Either way, I needed to get my butt out of the middle of the road.

My mind raced as I hurried to the sidewalk. *What's the last thing I remember? I was in the library and saw that odd glowing letter* L *on the cover of* Jane Eyre. *I touched it and—*

"Now then. Come along."

It was Mr. Briggs. I knew him. I mean, I didn't *know* him and didn't know *how* I knew him, but...but I did. He was Mr. Briggs, the attorney from *Jane Eyre*. He led me down the macadamized street.

"Wh-what are we doing?" I asked.

"He's asked for you, and you indicated you wanted to see him." He frowned down at me. "Have you changed your mind?"

"No." I reached out and took Briggs' arm—I needed the support, but I also craved proof he was real. He was. As real as anything in this place. Had I fallen? Hit my head? Was this a dream? If so, it was the most vivid I'd ever experienced.

Briggs escorted me into a prison and spoke briefly with a jailer, who then led us to a cell. I was behind Briggs, so I couldn't see inside the cell at first.

The jailer pinched my shoulder.

I yelped in surprise and glared at him. "What was that for?"

"You don't belong here." His voice was a menacing hiss; and when he bared his teeth at me, a silverfish darted through them.

The tingling started at my scalp and worked its way through my spine. Still, I managed to lift my head slightly. I inherently knew I couldn't show this creature any hint of fear.

Briggs moved aside, and I turned away from the jailer and stepped closer to the bars.

"Edward," I whispered. Edward Rochester, the brooding hero of *Jane Eyre*.

"Jane. Darling, Jane." He reached for my hands through the bars.

I put my hands out, and he squeezed them.

Staring into my eyes, he said, "Wait. You aren't—" He addressed Mr. Briggs then. "May we have a bit of privacy?"

"Of course. I'll be in the other room with the jailer." Mr. Briggs patted my forearm before walking away.

"Who are you?" Edward asked quietly.

"I'm Gia."

"Did Cooper send you?"

Cooper—the man who'd hired me as archivist for the Smithmore Manor library this morning.

"Yes," I said. Maybe Cooper had sent me, and maybe he hadn't, but *yes* seemed to be the safest answer under the circumstances.

Edward blew out a breath of relief. It wasn't pleasant. Didn't they have toothpaste in the 1840s? Gum? Mints? I'd have to look into that.

"What are you doing in prison?" I asked.

"I'm to be hanged in five days for the murder of my wife."

"Murder? No one killed Bertha. She committed suicide after setting the fire."

He shook his head. "There was no fire, and Bertha was murdered."

"You—?"

"No," he interrupted. "Not me. You need to find out who did kill her and work with Briggs to get me exonerated. I'm from your world; but if I die in this world, I'm dead in both." He paused. "Same goes for you."

I gulped. "That's good to know."

It wasn't, Reader. It wasn't good to know in the slightest.

"We have few allies here and many enemies."

"Oh, I've already made an enemy," I said. "The jailer pinched me! Then he told me I didn't belong here. And when I looked up at him, there was a silverfish in his mouth. Do you people not have toothpaste?"

"He is a silverfish. They destroy books. You're here to preserve the book—and, hopefully, my life."

"Okay, how do I—?"

"Time to go, Miss Eyre." Briggs had returned.

"Please," I said, "can't we have a few minutes more? I have so many questions."

"The jailer won't permit it. Perhaps we may return in a day or two."

"A day or two? We only have five!"

Edward pressed my hands before letting them go. "Cooper must have faith in you, so I do as well. Go and use the utmost caution."

I nodded. *What have I gotten myself into?*

* * *

Briggs helped me into a hansom cab and instructed the driver to take me to Thornfield Hall.

Thornfield Hall—the Rochester home. I tried to swallow the lump that had formed in my throat. *Wonder what awaits me there?*

"I have things to attend to in town, my dear, but I'll be around to check on you later this afternoon," he told me.

There weren't any silverfish in his mouth, as far as I could tell. I thanked him and was relieved for some time alone.

Taking a closer look at my outfit, I had to admit that the person who'd fashioned it had done an excellent job. It certainly felt authentic. The reticule hanging from my left wrist was gray with a floral bouquet embroidered on the front and tassels at the corners. I'd noticed the purse earlier but now took the opportunity to see what was inside—hopefully, a piece of hard candy for my uncomfortably dry mouth.

I untied the drawstring and pulled the fabric apart.

Inside was a small fan, some coins, a lace-edged handker-chief, and a folded piece of tan paper. Snatching the paper out of the purse, I opened it and read:

Gia, if you're reading this, you've taken your first journey into Literatia. Congratulations! No, you aren't crazy; you aren't dreaming; you aren't comatose; you aren't dead; you aren't whatever else you might believe you are. You're actually in another world—a book world—and you must recalibrate that world before the silverfish entirely destroy the book. But no worries. I have the utmost faith in your abilities. Fond regards, Cooper Wellingham

Staring down at my employer's words, I said aloud, "This *has* to be a dream."

The words on the note immediately disappeared and were replaced with: *It isn't. I already told you that.*

"Wait. I can talk with you using this paper?"

Again, like some sort of weird voice-to-text device that worked in reverse or backward or upside down or something, the paper was erased, and new words appeared.

In a way. I told you when you accepted the job this morning that you were taking on a challenging role. You indicated you enjoyed challenges.

"Well, yeah, but not sci-fi, world-hopping challenges that include people with silverfish in their teeth. This is way too out of the box for me."

Had I believed you were not up to the task, I'd have never allowed you to embark upon this journey. If you aren't recep-

tive, I need to pull you out and get someone inside who is willing to help Mr. Rochester immediately.

"I never said I wasn't willing to help Mr. Rochester." I huffed. "Of course, I am. I just—" I chewed on my lower lip for a second. "Get in here and help me already."

Unfortunately, I cannot. I'd be recognized immediately in Literatia, and the silverfish would work quickly to devour the book and everything in it. That includes Mr. Rochester and you in case you hadn't guessed.

"Mr. Rochester told me that if we die in the book, we die. Period. Am I getting hazardous duty pay for this gig? Because we never talked about my risk of dying. I figured my biggest threat would be a papercut."

Finish your task successfully, and you will be rewarded.

I wasn't making myself clear. I needed to reframe my question and stop being flippant. "What are the odds of my dying here?"

The words previously written faded out, but new words didn't come right away.

"Did you hear me?" I asked.

Low. Under all but the most extreme circumstances, I will be able to extricate you before you die.

"Oh." I slumped against my seat in relief. "And you can get Rochester out too, right?"

No. His life is in your hands.

"But he's your guy. He knew you sent me before *I* knew you sent me. You can't just leave him in there. In fact, why can't you take us both out of here now?"

I'm unable to remove Rochester. If I get you out, Rochester will die, and the literary classic Jane Eyre *will never have existed. That has farther-reaching ramifications in our world and in Literatia than you realize. I will ask you once again, are you up to this challenge?*

"I am."

Good.

"I'll keep this paper with me at all times so that I can communicate with you as necessary."

This is the only communication we can have until you return. If you were to be found with this paper, you'd be hanged as a witch.

"The last witch hanging in England took place in the late 1600s."

Trust me, they'll make an exception. Now, I'll leave you with a few words of clarification: Not everyone is who they seem or have the same personalities as those they originally embodied in the book. One of those characters killed Rochester's wife. Bring that person to justice, free Rochester, and you will be brought home. Godspeed.

Starting at one corner, the paper turned to ash. I realized Cooper was burning it on the other side. I brushed it onto the floor of the cab and watched it completely turn to dust.

This morning I'd started what I guessed would be a boring but nice job as an archivist at a gorgeous manor house in the hills of North Carolina. Now it wasn't even lunchtime, and I was responsible for a man's life, trying to avoid being killed myself, and tasked with keeping *Jane Eyre* safe for readers everywhere.

The cab came to a stop. I took out a coin and pulled the drawstring to close my reticule when I heard the driver climbing down from his seat.

"I thought I heard you talking," he said, upon opening the door and helping me out. "Me wife was a praying woman too."

I smiled. "Too bad she isn't here. I could use all the help I can get."

To either keep reading An Eyre of Mystery or to find more information on the rest of the series—including the free prequel, Saving Piglet, please visit the author's website at gayleleeson.com.

We hope you've enjoyed your foray into Literatia and that you'll continue to escape into books with us!

www.ingramcontent.com/pod-product-compliance
Lightning Source LLC
Chambersburg PA
CBHW050843180626
46814CB00007B/2606